WORDS
WE
DON'T
SAY

HYPERION
Los Angeles New York

First Edition, October 2018
10 9 8 7 6 5 4 3 2 1
FAC-020093-18229
Printed in the United States of America

Text is set in Adobe Caslon Pro/Fontspring
Designed by Jamie Alloy

Library of Congress Cataloging-in-Publication Data

Names: Reilly, K. J. (Writer of young adult fiction), author.
Title: Words we don't say / K.J. Reilly.
Description: First edition. • Los Angeles ; New York : Hyperion, 2018. •
Summary: "High school junior Joel Higgins grapples with the aftermath of a tragic loss as he tries to make sense of the problems he sees all around him with the help of banned books, Winnie-the-Pooh, a field of asparagus, and many pairs of socks"— Provided by publisher.
Identifiers: LCCN 2017060799 (print) •LCCN 2018010594 (ebook) •ISBN 9781368022750 (e-book) •ISBN 9781368016339 (hardcover)
Subjects: •CYAC: Coming of age—Fiction. •Homeless persons—Fiction. •Soup kitchens—Fiction. •Loss (Psychology)—Fiction. •Friendship—Fiction. • High schools—Fiction. •Schools—Fiction.
Classification: LCC PZ7.1.R4553 (ebook) •LCC PZ7.1.R4553 Som 2018 (print) • DDC [Fic]—dc23
LC record available at https://lccn.loc.gov/2017060799

Reinforced binding

Visit www.hyperionteens.com

SUSTAINABLE FORESTRY INITIATIVE Certified Sourcing
www.sfiprogram.org
SFI-00993

THIS LABEL APPLIES TO TEXT STOCK

For J. M., Kate, and Kenz, who kept me so busy reading books to them over the years that I neglected—until just recently—to write one of my own. And for River Flynn, who I look forward to reading to for many years to come.

1

SOMETIMES WE GAVE THEM NAMES.

We had to because they wouldn't tell us who they were.

Eli and I gave them made-up names just so we could identify them between ourselves. Besides, most were regulars who never missed a night, so we couldn't exactly *not* refer to them by one name or another.

They weren't mean names, either. And we never used the names we made up to their faces.

That wouldn't have been right, and we knew it.

This thing we did had *rules*.

Like dessert was only served twice a week.

And you had to eat a full meal to get it.

And the doors closed at 6:30 p.m. sharp.

And the new guys who didn't talk got fake names.

2

SOME OF THE GUYS WHO CAME IN

were real friendly.

Telling us their life stories and then what took them down. A lot of them, like the Colonel and Spindini, were veterans of wars that we hardly knew anything about. Some were addicts or alcoholics. Others were what Benj Kutchner, another eleventh grader who volunteered with us at the soup kitchen up on Hendricks Street on Wednesday nights, just called bat-shit crazy.

Which was ironic since pretty much our whole grade thought Benj Kutchner was bat-shit crazy on account of the fact that his mouth was unconnected to his brain. That, and the rumors floating around school that he poisoned his parents but the cops couldn't prove it and that's why he had to move here last summer to live with his aunt, who, if you listened to Alex B. Renner and his tribe of AP math geeks and wannabe tech titans, was apparently not looking too good herself these days.

But most of the guys who showed up at the soup kitchen weren't veterans or alcoholics or addicts or mentally ill. They were just normal guys who'd lost the cosmic luck lottery. As Spindini, one of the regulars and the resident philosopher, summed it up one night when some bad shit went down and the cops had to come and haul the Colonel out in handcuffs, “Fuck it, man, sometimes life just ain’t fair.”

And goddamn, but he got that right.

A FEW OF THE GUYS WHO DID TALK

offered us advice.

Heaps of it.

In between bites of mashed potatoes and green beans, those affirmative statements to "do this" and the warnings to "don't do that" poured out of them with such force it was like they were holding fire hoses and we were buildings about to go up in smoke. Hoping maybe they would say something that just might keep one of us from ending up homeless and hungry one day with demons so big and so bad that there'd be no way to get out from under them. It was as if they knew that the flames of life were licking at all of our combustible surfaces and if they could just say the right thing they could extinguish them before it was too late and we were nothing but the charred remains of someone who was something once.

Or could have been.

But it was like some of them, the ones who didn't speak, were scared quiet. Like if they said anything out loud, even their own names, the little bit they were holding together would split wide open. When it came to those guys, I didn't know what they were dealing with, or who they were, or how to approach them. So when they came through the line I just gave them a plate of food and a smile and a polite nod. But Eli always made like the soup kitchen was a real restaurant, and they were just regular customers, so she tried real hard and was extra nice like she was working toward a big tip or knew something the rest of us didn't. She was always acting like everything was really okay even when it really wasn't and was always saying sweet stuff like, "Hope you like the meat loaf." Or, "The pasta looks really good tonight." Or, "Here's an extra piece of cake."

She had to whisper real low about the cake, too, because old Mrs. Torrington, the lady who ran the soup kitchen, had strict rules about handing out more than one serving per. That's just how Mrs. T said it, too, with her finger wagging and pointing right at Eli, 'cause she knew who had the soft heart, "Only one serving per." Sometimes even adding "Eli" to the end of that sentence just in case any of the volunteers didn't know who she was talking to or wagging her finger at.

Said that every time we gave out seconds it meant that someone else went hungry.

Mrs. Torrington had a point. Some nights we ran out of everything—not just cake—and then we had to turn people away. Believe me, none of us wanted to be the one to make the cutoff in that line of hungry people and lock the doors, or decide instead that maybe one or two more could slide through and we could scrape together just a couple of more meals. So Mrs. T had to pull the doors closed and bolt them tight herself while the rest of us looked at the floor or glanced up hoping not to make eye contact with anyone as wc did some quick math on how many were being turned away on that particular night, knocked down yet another notch, cold and hungry.

It was mostly men in the soup kitchen line snaking toward Main. It would have been way worse if more of them were women—or kids. That's just a fact.

I don't know why that is. But I don't know much of anything, so you wouldn't want to come looking to me for answers to that or anything else. Unless you wanted to know how to repair a transmission or change the oil in your truck. Shit like that was clean and simple and I knew it cold.

4

ME AND ELI WERE AT THE SOUP KITCHEN

one night a week to fulfill a community service requirement at our school, Calf City High, just a few miles north of New York City and a few giant steps west of the Hudson River in Rockland County.

In eleventh grade, one full semester of community service was required if you wanted to graduate. No negotiating either. Believe me, kids tried.

Eli picked the soup kitchen because she liked feeding people. And I picked the soup kitchen because I liked watching Eli do just about anything at all.

Sometimes life could be that simple.

But in my book, not often enough.

The regulars lined up early. Started milling around the doors at about four o'clock, and back on our first night of volunteering, Eli had whispered to me, "That's what the cats always did at Shady Brook."

"I remember," I said, knowing that she didn't mean anything awful by it despite how it sounded 'cause Eli's never said anything bad about anyone or anything in her whole life. It's just that when we were in elementary school, the janitors and lunch ladies used to leave food for the stray cats by the back door of the cafeteria at 1:00 p.m. and those cats showed up early and hung around the door, too.

Those early birds at the soup kitchen would eventually form an orderly line that grew longer and longer as they waited for the doors to open at 5:00 p.m. sharp. A line that reached all the way to Mr. Easton's fix-it shop on the corner of Main and Hendricks on most nights, and probably stretched farther than that on more nights than any of us liked to think. But we couldn't see the end from inside where we were standing.

"It hurts your heart to see this," Eli said over and over again, referring to the number of people waiting to eat, or some new guy, or a regular, or the doors that were bolted shut when there were still faces peering in from the other side.

She was right about that.

And she was right about a whole bunch of other stuff, too.

I MET ROOSTER ON WEDNESDAY NIGHT,

first week in March.

That's not his real name, of course. It's one of those made-up names Eli and I came up with. He showed up real late that night, around 6:15 or so, then he hung around outside for a bit before he tamped down whatever it was that was holding him back and mustered up the courage to come in.

Eli saw him before me, said, "Here comes a straggler. Hope we still have cake."

I looked up and saw the guy just standing there outside the entrance. Then I looked at the clock 'cause we were gonna close soon and I started hoping he would hurry. Sort of willing him in through the door.

Rooster was big, real big, and wearing more layers of clothes than you'd think were possible—or necessary—even at the tail end of a New York winter. He finally got up the guts and pulled open the door and stepped inside. Just stood there with his red face and matted hair and those scared blue eyes that darted around the room real nervous-like, then he'd glance back outside every few seconds at the shopping cart he had parked on the sidewalk like he was afraid to leave it.

They were all afraid to leave their stuff. Mrs. Torrington told us that at orientation six weeks back. That they were all afraid someone would steal it. She said that even though it wasn't worth anything to anyone else, it was all they had.

"I vote that if he doesn't tell us his name, we call him Rooster," I said to Eli, leaning in close, not just because I liked to—and I liked to—but so no one else could hear.

"Rooster? Where'd you get that one?" Eli whispered back, her breath all warm and inviting on my cheek.

"After Rooster Cogburn in *True Grit*," I said. "Played by Jeff Bridges. This guy looks just like him."

"Which is how?" Eli asked.

"Like a big old unkempt grizzly bear."

"Well, I'll just have to take your word for that," Eli said, as she slapped some rice and beans onto a plate for the next guy through the line, "as I haven't seen that movie."

"But you see the bear, Eli. Tell me you see the bear," I teased, and that got her to laugh.

"Yes, Joel, I see the bear."

We always named the guys who didn't talk after characters we'd seen in movies. We had ourselves a Red from *The Shawshank Redemption* and a Gandalf from Lord of the Rings, and from the looks of it, we had a Rooster now, too.

I went right over to him and said, "Welcome, sir," and knew right off the bat that he wasn't going to talk.

He looked scared of me—and I'm not someone to be scared of. I'm all of five foot eight inches tall, hoping on five foot nine and praying for five foot ten like it was the difference between fixing flats and tuning up SUVs at my pop's gas station for the rest of my life or signing a contract to be a guard for the New York Knicks.

Like I could play for the Knicks even if I were seven feet tall.

I mean, I can't shoot hoops for shit or dribble a ball between my legs or drive toward the basket with some tall-ass, jacked-up ass-lete running me down, but the way I figured it in my head, those were two inches that had the power to change just about everything in my life. The thing of it was, by my calculation, those couple of inches wouldn't just keep me pumping gas and out of the NBA so to speak, they would keep me from Eli. I was struggling with the colossal problem that Eli was five foot ten and not likely to notice me outside of school and the soup kitchen as more than just some stupid kid she's gone to school with her whole life if I was way down here and she was way up there.

Now, you'd think seeing what I saw at Hendricks Street on Wednesday nights would make me think being short was a problem I could work around, but you'd be wrong. Even after slinging hash in a soup kitchen and seeing just about the worst the world could dish out, I *still* managed to feel sorry for myself because I fell just a couple of tragic inches short of my ideal height and a shot at a girl.

I'm guessing that if I were offered the choice, I would probably have left half the world to starve just for those two goddamned inches and a shot at Eli.

That doesn't say much about Joel Higgins, now, does it?

But if you saw Eli, you'd understand where I'm coming from. It's not that she was Victoria's Secret kind of pretty either, she was just *my kind of pretty* and she had this way about her. It was like she really believed that she could fix anything and everything would be okay if she just stuck with it and tried hard enough.

I'd known Eli since first grade, had a crush on her since fifth, and been flat out in love with her since seventh, but the sad truth is that in all that time I hadn't gotten up the courage to ask her out or tell her how I felt. Then, after the thing that happened last year, Eli walked right back to the lunch table near the emergency door and trash cans and the posters for the Heimlich maneuver and CPR that were taped to the wall in the wayback of the cafeteria where me and my friend Andy always sat, and she set her tray down right across from me in the empty space.

She just asked, "Would it be okay if I sit here, Joel?" but not until after she sat down.

I said, "You don't have to—"

But she interrupted me and said, "Of course I don't have to. I want to."

And I pretty much knew that that wasn't true, but I nodded my head anyway.

From that first day on, Eli sat with me at lunch in Andy's old spot. Never once said anything to make a big deal out of it or acted like she was doing me a favor either. That's just the kind of person she is. But we never talked much. I pretty much sat there thinking about everything wrong with the world and Eli worked on writing out lists of everything she was happy about and all the things she could fix.

That night at the soup kitchen, I reassured the new guy—who we decided to call Rooster—that I would watch his stuff. Then Eli came over and she was real sweet and looking pretty with a great big smile and her hair pulled way up on top of her head in a ponytail that was crisscrossed into a braid and she got him to follow right after her so she could plate him some food. He ate it real fast, too. Cake and all. Kept checking the door, though, and I'd wave back at him from outside where I was babysitting his cart to let him know that everything on my end was A-OK.

We weren't supposed to, but we did stuff like that—babysat their carts and shit so they could eat. Ten minutes in, Mrs. T popped her head outside and said, "Joel, you doing all right?"

And I wanted to say, "Fuck no. Things are not the least bit all right. There's bad shit going on everywhere and a room full of hungry people and most of them have nowhere to live and a whole bunch of them have shopping carts full of garbage they can't part with. So no. Things are not all right out here."

But I basically said, "Yes, Mrs. T. I've got this. Just getting some fresh air."

And she said, "Sure you are, Joel. Sure you are."

Most of the guys came into the soup kitchen early and ate real slow. It was a chance to sit down and warm up. But Rooster, he apparently had things to do and places to go. He was in late and out fast that night and every Wednesday night after that, too.

Things were just humming along until the third Saturday in March when I was walking along the old dirt road by the cemetery up in the hill section of town. I was headed down to the village for no particular reason other than I couldn't stand spending another second listening to my pop scream at the TV because the Yankees were losing in the fifth inning of a preseason game and not taking his advice to "pull the goddamned pitcher," when I saw Rooster with his shopping cart heading back into the woods behind the Richardsons' farm. Just caught a glimpse of him as he cut in on an old path we used to use as kids, then he disappeared into the trees and brush. Had a hell of a time maneuvering his shopping cart because of the uneven ground and busted wheel, but it was Rooster all right. I deduced that there was a good chance that he was living up in those woods. No other reason to go there. Even for someone who might well be, as Benj Kutchner would say, bat-shit crazy.

I decided to check it out for myself the next day.

Which was my first mistake.

My second mistake was way worse.

In fact, my mistakes were what Mr. Monty, my eleventh-grade math teacher, called *progressing geometrically*, which he explained by saying that if you started with a penny and doubled it every day, in one month you'd have $10.7 million. When he explained the penny thing, Benj Kutchner was sitting right behind me and he leaned forward and said, "Hey, Higgins? Can I borrow a penny?" Then he whispered, "That's what happens to problems, too." And I figured that if he really did kill his parents, he would know. Mr. Monty called it a form of compounding, said it was a good thing, but later on Benj called it *sequential worsening*. I figured that Benj was right; things just started to get worse and worse once you made one mistake. And I imagined that you could go from one wrong to 10.7 million wrongs in thirty days just as if those problems were compounding pennies if you doubled your output each day. Something I learned wasn't too hard to do if you were Joel Higgins and you were sequentially screwing up.

* * *

On that orientation night at the Hendricks Street soup kitchen Mrs. T warned us not to nose into their lives or try to save them. Said a whole bunch of docs had failed at that already so there was no point in our trying. "We're just here to feed 'em," she said, "not fix 'em."

I wished I'd listened to Mrs. T that day. Wished it a whole lot since that third Saturday in March. But something my pop always said stuck with me through all this. He usually didn't say much. Not much of a talker, my pop, unless you counted all the screaming he did at the TV when the Yankees were losing. But when things got real bad, he'd revert to his quiet self, shake his head back and forth slowly, and say under his breath, "It is what it is." Like whatever it was, it was a damned shame, but just like a blown-out tire or a seized-up engine, it was flat-out, undeniably unfixable.

And that just about summed up what happened between Rooster and me. We geometrically progressed to flat-out unfixable.

6

HERE'S A BIT MORE

you should know about me:

My pop's named Jackson.

My mom's named Mary.

I have one brother who's five years old and we call Jace.

Basically the things that I am good at, they don't teach in high school.

I don't actually know what the things that I am good at are yet, 'cause other than playing video games or pulling a car engine apart and putting it back together again, I pretty much haven't found any. But I know one thing for damned sure, it's not the trombone or Euclidean geometry or diagramming sentences, or poetry.

Or gym.

Or French.

Definitely not French.

I can't parlez-vous for shit.

Math is pretty much a dead zone, too.

To give you an example, here's something Mr. Monty wrote on the board in math class:

The average of four numbers is five less than the average of the three numbers that remain after one has been eliminated. If the eliminated number is 2, what is the average of the four numbers?

Even before anyone else finished reading the problem, some freshman called out, "The answer's seventeen."

Here's what I was thinking about when that freshman was figuring that the average of four numbers that is five less than the average of the three numbers that remain after one has been eliminated when the one that was eliminated was 2, is 17:

Eli.
Rocket ships.
Eli.
NBA 2K18.
Eli.
The pretzels in the cafeteria.
Eli.

Pretty much in that order.

Eli because she's Eli and rocket ships because a SpaceX Falcon rocket just blew up at launch and *NBA 2K18* because it has cool dribbling and hook-shot features and I was going to play it all summer with Andy but that got ruined because of the thing that happened and the pretzels in the cafeteria because they should have more salt on them and also be free because sometimes you want more than one and you don't have enough money with you, and then Eli again and again, just because she's Eli.

Then when Mr. Monty started writing another meaningless-worthless-boring-ridiculous math problem on the blackboard that he said would be on the SAT, I started thinking that they should redesign the entire school transportation system and everyone should walk to school until eleventh grade and then they should give all of us our own cars with the money they saved on buses and bus drivers and bus headquarters and bus insurance and bus cleaning and bus gas and bus tune-ups and bus everything because the school bus is like an insane asylum on wheels and having your own car is cool.

I was thinking, maybe Corvette Stingrays for the seniors and Camaros for the juniors.

Then Mr. Monty said, "Joel, are you paying attention?" And I said, "No fucking way. I have far better things to think about."

But I left off the "fucking" part and the "no" part and the "I have far better things to think about" part, too.

So, I pretty much said, "Yes, sir. I am paying close attention."

Then he asked me to factor the equation he had written on the board. This is what it looked like:

$$\mathbf{x^2 — 3 = 2x}$$

I was thinking, there's no way I know how to do that. And then I looked down at what I had written in my notebook so it looked like maybe I was trying to factor the equation and I had figured out that

114 Corvette Stingrays (that was how many seniors we had) at $55,450 apiece would cost the school district just about $6,321,300, and 97 Camaros for the junior class at $25,905 each would cost $2,512,785, so together that was $8,834,085. I had recently looked it up on my phone and I knew that the whole transportation budget for the school district was just about exactly $8 million, so that basically meant we would have to be given less expensive cars.

Then I said, "With regard to factoring, sir, I've got nothing."

That annoying freshman had his hand up again, and he was frantically waving as if an alien had planted an exploding math pod in his head. Mr. Monty called on him and the kid said, "The answer is negative one and three." He hadn't even used a pencil to find it and we all knew he was right. I mean, come on, he was a freshman in eleventh-grade math.

Then Mr. Monty looked back over at me and he made that face that all of my teachers made when it was clear they weren't getting through to me and they wished that they were. Or maybe it was just that they were wishing that I was a different person or in a different class, or living in a different country like Estonia or Yemen or Kyrgyzstan, or maybe back in third grade, where they could start over and correct some of these problems before they even started.

Here are a few other things you should know about me:

Last December I got the lowest score you could get on the SAT. Apparently, the only thing I got right was my name.

I'm always surrounded by people, but I have no real friends. Not even one. At least not anymore.

The things most kids care about don't matter to me.

And I think everyone I know has a horrible illness and is going to die any minute. Especially me.

Plus, I'm not tall enough or big enough for sports, except for the horrible sports like gymnastics and wrestling. I do not want to roll around with sweaty guys on a sweaty mat or hang from rings in tights. I *would* like to roll around on a sweaty mat with Eli, especially if she was wearing tights—or no tights. Either way. In her case, I'm pretty flexible on the tights. But she's not in my gym class, so that's pretty much not an option.

I got suspended in the beginning of the year for hitting someone on the school bus, which is frowned upon. But believe me, the kid deserved it. It was the second week of school and Benj Kutchner had just gotten on the bus at the corner of Adams and Hillsdale, and Anthony Pittsfield, who is known to everyone as the Pittster because he sweats so much that his shirts always have wet circles under the armpits, stuck his foot out on purpose and tripped Kutchner for no reason and he landed flat on his face in the bus aisle. I was sitting two rows back and saw the whole thing, so I hopped up and decked the guy. Didn't even really know Benj then either. I mean, I knew he was the new kid who probably killed his parents and that he was really annoying but that's no reason to trip someone.

I also have 212 unsent text messages on my phone to Mr. Redman, the principal of Calf City High School—or CC, as we call it for short.

I have 454 unsent text messages to Eli.

And 235 unsent text messages to Andy.

The whole reason that I have all those unsent text messages stored on my phone is because Mrs. Wilson, the school psychologist who has no idea what she is doing, who I had to go see last year after the thing that happened with Andy, suggested that I write whatever I was thinking about in a journal, and I said, "No fucking way."

Except without the "fucking" part.

Which pretty much means I said, "No way." Politely.

As in, "I don't think that would work for me, Mrs. Wilson, but thank you for the suggestion."

But then I just started writing text messages on my phone like I was going to send them, except I stopped before I hit send and instead I hit save to draft. I got the idea after I saw this girl on a rerun of the TV show *Shark Tank*, which is where some people go when they invent shit and start businesses and try to get investors to give them money. This girl—who was sixteen years old just like me—invented an app called ReThink for kids' phones and tablets and computers, so if they typed anything foul smelling and atrocious, or just flat-out nasty, a message would pop up on their screen:

ReThink! Don't say things that you may regret later!

It's like a pause button for brains that don't have pause buttons, which is pretty much everyone I know in high school. Anyway, the girl who invented the app said that she did a test and 93 percent of the time—or maybe it was 87.2 percent or 89.3 percent of the time, I can't remember—kids deleted the bad message when that ReThink warning popped up.

So basically she invented a way to put duct tape over kids' nasty mouths and help stop cyberbullying, and when I saw that show, I decided that I was a total loser because I didn't invent a way for kids to stop hurting each other. And then I decided that I could write text messages and not send them at all but not delete them either. It was sort of like I invented my own app to talk to people I wanted to talk to but couldn't talk to for a whole variety of reasons that I won't get into. That meant that I didn't have to ReThink because I never hit send, which meant that I could pretty much say anything that I wanted to say without worrying about ReThinking, which would be a pretty cool app if you think about it and probably if I did a test 93 percent or maybe 87.2 percent or 89.3 percent of kids who used it would like it. I mean, who wouldn't like to say anything they fucking wanted to, to anyone they fucking wanted to say it to, but then not say it and not delete it but just save it for later so you could see how screwed up and weird you were at some future date?

So I pretty much kept a journal like Mrs. Wilson said, just on my phone.

I'm thinking about maybe taking the idea to *Shark Tank*. I think all of the nice sharks would like it. Except the old, bald guy they call Mr. Wonderful just to be ironic, because he's mean and wouldn't get it. Plus he says, "You're dead to me," if someone won't take his deal, which is no different than bullying. He probably sat in the back of the school bus in high school and picked on kids who had hair. Which was pretty much everyone.

Which is why we shouldn't have buses at all.

Because of Mr. Wonderful on *Shark Tank* we should all be driving Corvettes and Camaros.

TEXT FROM JOEL TO PRINCIPAL REDMAN 1:17 p.m.

About my end the bus campaign.

If we can't get the Stingrays, classic Mustangs are cool too.

TEXT FROM JOEL TO ANDY 2:14 p.m.

There's a new kid in school this year. He probably killed his parents but you would like him even though he's really annoying. And maybe a felon.

They had pizza at lunch.

I had two pieces and a pretzel and plain milk.

They don't have chocolate milk anymore. You would hate it.

TEXT FROM JOEL TO PRINCIPAL REDMAN 3:59 p.m.

Gym sucks. We should do something about gym too.

As long as we're fixing stuff.

TEXT FROM JOEL TO ELI 1:15 a.m.

I pretty much love you. I mean, I know you don't love me but maybe you should know how I feel. Just in case.

It's Joel by the way.

I mean, just in case you don't have my number saved in your phone.

Joel Higgins.

7

LIKE MOST THINGS, THE THING WITH ROOSTER

started as nothing, then became something real fast.

The day after I saw him heading into the woods, I walked back there myself. The Richardson place was close to a hundred acres and they raised chickens and grew apples on real old trees with big old scraggly limbs like the ones you might see in a spooky kids' cartoon at Halloween. Real quiet, too. A sort of run-down gentleman's farm where the gentleman's really old and not up to keeping after the place and not quite rich enough or interested enough to pay a whole bunch of someone elses to do it for him.

Back in the woods, just a few hundred yards from the tree line, I came across a shanty behind one of the Richardsons' old barns. The barn was way past needing paint and was courting a date with a bulldozer if you asked me, but the shanty, I figured, could be felled by the driving gust of a whisper. It was easy to find, too, since Rooster wouldn't leave that damned shopping cart of his behind and it left wheel marks in the brush that didn't take high-level tracking skills to identify. Plus, he had a couple of backup shopping carts full of all kinds of shit stashed back there as well. His place was slapped up with a few pieces of plywood and sheet metal and a few two-by-fours and old fence posts that were lashed together with a whole lot of rusty wire and rope by someone who had clearly not been thinking right. Inside was nothing but a dirt floor knee-high in garbage. And I mean *garbage*. It was a rat's nest of a hovel that made me feel even worse than I thought it was possible for me to feel about anything or anyone.

What Rooster had in the woods behind the Richardsons' place was as bad as it gets.

He wasn't there, but I left him a few things by the door that I thought he could use. I'd brought some canned food from my mom's pantry, the kind that had pull-off lids, figuring that he probably didn't have a can opener. And I left him a pair of my socks because I read that socks were real important to homeless guys. I don't know why socks and not blankets or shoes or anything else but I brought the socks and a toothbrush, too, even though teeth were likely not a top priority, considering. Just left all the stuff by the entrance without actually going inside. Figured this was his home and I hadn't been invited in.

Not that I wanted to be invited in, but still.

Then I just walked back out on the same path I came in on, and headed on my way.

8

WHAT HAD STARTED AS A CURIOSITY BECAME

a habit.

Obsession, really.

And real fast, too.

I started stopping by Rooster's a couple of times a week to drop stuff off for him. My mom kept asking me, "Joel, where are all your socks?" And I would play dumb and act like the washer ate them—we all know the washer eats them—or suggest that they walked off on their own in violent protest over the nasty condition of my feet.

Not sure if I was doing this for Rooster or for me, but either way that's what I did.

Got me in some trouble at school, too. Fuckin' Benj Kutchner saw some cans of food in my backpack one day and he reached in and grabbed a fifteen-ounce can of Libby's fruit cocktail, pulled open the pop-top lid, and slurped it down right there in third-period Chemistry, right before the teacher showed up for class.

"What the hell you got in here, Joel?" he asked as he nudged my backpack with his foot, heavy syrup running down his chin. "A food pantry?"

Then Alex B. Renner—who no one called Alex because he went by his full name at all times—said, "Be quiet, turds. I'm scoring my practice math SAT."

Smack Hemmings ignored him and yelled, "Joel's a fruit cocktail." And Mikey Malone said, "Shut the hell up, dipwads." Then Alex B. Renner said, "Boom! 750!" And pretty much everyone wanted to poke his eyes out with his protractor or strangle him with his laptop cord.

I wish it would have ended there, but things went downhill on account of the fact that I punched Benj in the face just as Mr. Klein walked into the classroom catching only the tail end of the dispute. Mr. Klein just saw the reaction, not the cause, which as a chemistry teacher he should have recognized as problematic. But he didn't, and he tagged me as the guilty party.

My pop had to come down to pick me up from Redman's office because the school basically operated under the teachers-intervene-to-fix-everything method of conflict resolution while my pop taught me the take-it-outside-and-work-it-out-between-yourselves technique. From my experience, as long as two guys were evenly matched, my pop's way tended to work out better than if someone made you behave some way that you didn't want to.

Whenever I had an argument with my brother, Jacey, I would joke and say to my pop, "Can we take it outside and work it out ourselves?" Not really meaning it of course 'cause Jace was just a little kid and I would never hit him or most people for that matter except under the most extreme circumstances. Pop would say, "No, you're not evenly matched," and I would look at him and then he would wink and say, "Jace would take you in a second, Joel." Jacey would be so proud he would forget what we were fighting about and I would scoop him up and race around the living room holding him upside down with him screaming and having the best time of his life and Pop would say, "Take it outside, both of you," meaning the horsing around, not the fight. And then he'd add, "I mean it. Outside. You two are blocking the TV," and the whole fight thing between Jace and me would be over and Pop would be back to yelling at the Yankees and Jace would go back to playing with his trucks and I'd go to my room to type text messages to Eli and Andy and Principal Redman that I had no intention of ever sending.

Anyway, under the teachers-intervene-to-fix-everything method, I was suspended for three days for fighting. Benj got to lie down in the nurse's office with an ice pack on his face, and some freshman girl brought him lunch and he didn't get punished at all.

I asked Principal Redman before my pop and me left his office if I could still go do my community service at the soup kitchen the next day, basically neglecting to bring to his attention the fact that Benj Kutchner would be there, too. Redman said yes after stumbling a bit at first. He seemed rightfully impressed on account of the fact that even though I had just punched someone in the face I was apparently still a good person. But that was only because he didn't know my real motivation for doing community service was seeing Eli.

Then in the school parking lot my pop, who hadn't said much of anything in that meeting except, "I'll take Joel home and have a talk with him," said, "What on earth were you doin' hittin' Benj Kutchner? You know that boy ain't right in the head."

I said, "He stole my fruit cocktail," and regretted it the moment it came out of my mouth.

Pop just looked at me in his strong, silent way like one of the heroes from real old movies, like John Wayne or Steve McQueen or Paul Newman, one of those guys who didn't talk much but knew his way around right and wrong. Then he climbed into his truck and fired up the engine. Apparently he didn't want to pursue a conversation about fruit cocktail or anything else that was likely to make no sense whatsoever to someone not on the giving or receiving end of that punch.

If you think about it, what was I doing with a can of fruit cocktail in the first place, and what was Benj Kutchner doing stealin' it?

The whole thing made no sense.

TEXT FROM JOEL TO ELI 3:24 a.m.

I know that I pretty much break stuff and you pretty much fix stuff but maybe that would work because opposites attract.

I could try breaking less stuff maybe.
Or you could break stuff and I could fix stuff.
Either way.
I'm good with both.

TEXT FROM JOEL TO ANDY 3:37 a.m.

Okay, I have a bunch of new symptoms. All of them nasty. According to WebMD it's either a parasite, phlebitis, or a pulmonary embolism.

Probably all three.

Just so you know.

9

THE NEXT AFTERNOON

at 3:30 I was already in the back of the soup kitchen with Mrs. T setting up for dinner when Eli showed up.

I walked out of the pantry carrying a stack of plates just as Eli walked in. As she was hanging up her jacket she said, "Benj isn't coming tonight because his face hurts and he's supposed to put ice on it every fifteen minutes." Then she added, "You shouldn't hit anyone, Joel."

I put the stack of plates down and said, "I know that, Eli."

"Then why'd you do it?"

I couldn't tell her about Rooster and the food or Benj slurping down the fruit cocktail, so I just said something about the fact that sometimes you have to take a stand when something isn't right. And Eli looked at me fiery mad and said, "That's what I'm doing now. Taking a stand for something that's not right. Someone, somewhere along the way, must have told you that it's wrong to hit people."

"No matter what?"

"Yes. No matter what."

"So what if—"

"Don't do a what-if, Joel."

"I can do a what-if, you brought it up. *What if* you and I are walking down a dark alleyway and five men jump us and they have guns pointed right at us and one of them says, 'We're going to shoot both of you in one minute.' Can I hit them then, Eli? The five guys with the guns?"

"That's not a fair example."

"Why not?

"Because."

"No, *because*. You said it's wrong to hit people *no matter what*. Well, that's a *what*."

She didn't answer.

"Come on, tell me. Can I hit them, Eli?"

"You mean to say that if you and I are walking down a dark alley and five men jump out with guns and one of them says he will shoot us in one minute, you would actually consider hitting them?"

I slowly nodded my head.

Then I started to gloat.

Stupid, stupid mistake.

Eli just shook her head from side to side like I was the stupidest person she had ever met and then as she headed toward the kitchen I called after her, "Well, would *you* hit them?"

Eli just turned around and looked at me with that same you're-such-a-dumb-fuck-I-can't-even-respond expression on her face, and then she finally said, "What?"

"Would you hit them? I mean, even if I got us killed, at least I tried and in case we are ever walking down a dark alley together I want to know if you'll have my back."

Eli continued to look stupefied.

"Well?" I said.

"No. I would not hit them, Joel. First of all, I would avoid the back alley and if I *was* that stupid and I did walk down one I would try to talk my way out of the situation." Then she paused and added, "And I would have faith. That God would help me."

I was thinking, *God? Here we go again with God,* and I threw my hands up 'cause me and Eli had had this God battle a couple of times before and it did not go well. "You're betting on the same guy who sent the five men with guns to shoot you? You're going to wait for Him to bail you out?"

"If my choice was the creator of the entirety of the universe or you and your juvenile fists, no offense, but I'd go with Him." Then she paused for a beat and added, "Or Her." Eli turned and marched back to the kitchen, pushed the door open, and got to work helping Mrs. T with the coffee and tea setup while I stood there like the dumb fuck I apparently was with my mouth hanging open.

We didn't talk any further until later that night when a new guy showed up and I went over and whispered to her, "Let's give him a name. Who do you think he looks like?"

Eli was still pissed off and said she didn't want to play, so I said, "I'm sorry."

She said, "For what?"

I said, "For hitting Benj."

She didn't say anything.

"And for the God comment," I added.

"It's still not okay," she said and then she stormed off.

I called after her, "I know that."

And I did.

But Eli had God and I didn't.

So we were fundamentally different.

She believed in Him—or Her—and I believed that everything was on Me.

TEXT FROM JOEL TO PRINCIPAL REDMAN 2:04 a.m.

You should retire Andy's locker number like the
Yankees did for Lou Gehrig's #4 jersey.
Andy had locker #624 In the front hall in case you don't know.
Andy Westfield. Locker #624.

You remember Andy. Right?

TEXT FROM JOEL TO ELI 2:47 a.m.

Remember when we were in seventh grade at Family Fun Night and you got up on the stage before the whole school and all the parents and sang the Celine Dion song "My Heart Will Go On" and you couldn't sing and it was really bad? I was really scared that everyone would laugh but you meant it so much that all the moms started to cry and everyone stood up and clapped like you just won best new artist at the Grammys.

That was it for me. That was pretty much the
first time I fell in love with you.

I was like, holy shit. I could never do that.

10

WHEN I GOT TO HOMEROOM

on Monday after my suspension, Mr. McGuire held up a pass for me and said that I had to go see Mrs. Wilson, the school psychologist, for something he called "mediation and resolution."

I knew Mrs. Wilson pretty well on account of what I went through last year when everyone was worried about me. It wasn't that I had done something wrong, it was just one of those things that fell under the category of *really bad shit happens sometimes and it sucks.*

When I got to Mrs. Wilson's office, she said, "Hi, Joel," and Benj was sitting right there in front of her desk looking at his phone. Mrs. Wilson had a few books piled up and our folders out on her desk, and she basically told us that she wanted to make sure that now that we had some time to cool off there were no hard feelings and I wasn't gonna go and hit Mr. Kutchner anymore.

That's what she called him, "Mr. Kutchner." And she kept saying shit like, "conflict resolution," and "active listening," and "adjudication," and "conciliatory," and "peace dividends," and "emotional restitution," like that meant anything to either one of us. But as for when

Mrs. Wilson asked me directly if I would be hitting Mr. Kutchner again, I just said, "That depends," and she looked mighty mad on account of the fact that most kids who just got suspended for fighting would say that they wouldn't hit anyone ever again in their whole lives even if it was a flat-out lie. They wouldn't make the "no hitting" contingent on something. But Joel Higgins was still pretty pissed off at Mr. Kutchner. I had just spent three days fixing flat tires and rebuilding transmissions and putting on brake pads down at the station with my pop, which is way harder than sitting in school waiting for the hot pretzels to go on sale in the cafeteria or the next time I would get to see Eli walk by. Plus, I figured since Benj knew there was a good chance I had food in my backpack he was gonna be like a raccoon with his sights on a Dumpster.

While Mrs. Wilson was mulling over her plan of attack on what to say to the kid who just said that he might very well hit someone in the future depending on what that person did, she sat back in her chair and pursed her lips. I was thinking that whatever she was supposed to say probably wasn't printed right there in one of the brand-new guidance counselor books of things to say to kids who were in a fight that she had open on her desk and she was going to have to come up with something impromptu on her own. But before she did, Benj turned and looked at me and asked, "Joel, are you going to take Driver's Ed this semester?" and I said, "Yes." Then Benj asked, "Want to sit together in English today?" and I said, "Only if you leave my backpack alone," then he said, "That depends on what you have in there," and I jumped on him with a quick, "No, it doesn't." Then I said that he had to respect my stuff and stealing is stealing and I'm not someone he wanted to mess with or bully and that if he did it again he was gonna be sorry. And then I said that there were rules in this world and he needed to follow them and then Benj said he was sorry about the fruit cocktail.

It got real quiet for a few minutes and then Benj asked, "Can we still be friends?"

And I looked at the floor and said, "We were never friends."

He said, "I know. But still, can we hang out in the hallway and joke sometimes like we usually do?"

And I said, "Okay."

Then I said that I was sorry that I hit him but not really because he deserved it and then Mrs. Wilson looked at us like we weren't even speaking English and she coughed a little and pretended to read the papers in her folders, which were probably about how teachers should intervene to fix everything, and then she said, "Well, it sounds to me like things here are settled."

But it sounded like more of a question than a statement of fact, and I was gonna say as long as Benj keeps his paws out of my backpack because there are hungry people in the world and I can only take so much food from home without my mom noticing, but then I saw Benj's bright orange socks and I said, "I'll be your friend if you give me your socks." Mrs. Wilson sighed and threw the folder she was holding down on her desk because even though she probably has a degree in advanced adolescent thinking, our conversation confirmed that she had absolutely no idea how kids think.

Then while Kutchner was busy taking off his socks, Mrs. Wilson asked if either of us wanted to come back for another session next week. When Benj didn't answer I just said, "No, thank you. I think we're good."

Then Mrs. Wilson said, "So you're not going to hit Mr. Kutchner again, right, Joel?" And I said, "That depends."

At which point Mrs. Wilson just threw her hands up in the air and said, "I did not hear that." Then she gave us a pass and the bell rang and Benj and I walked to English together because that was the class we both had next.

TEXT FROM JOEL TO ANDY 12:10 a.m.

I'm sorry that I beat your best score at Grand Theft Auto. That wasn't fair. I won't play it again ever.

TEXT FROM JOEL TO ANDY 12:11 a.m.

Okay, I smashed the controller. Like, fucking killed it. Jackson's pissed. I said I didn't do it. But I think he knows. Jacey is five and doesn't smash shit. And my mom's the only other person in the house. I mean, come on.

TEXT FROM JOEL TO ANDY 12:13 a.m.

The school might be buying the whole junior class Camaros. I think I'll get black or red hot.

TEXT FROM JOEL TO ANDY 12:14 a.m.

Or maybe silver ice metallic. Silver's cool.

TEXT FROM JOEL TO ANDY 12:14 a.m.

With rally stripes and fender hash marks.

TEXT FROM JOEL TO ELI 2:06 a.m.

The second time I fell in love with you was the next time I saw you. And then it was pretty much every time I saw you after that.

11

WE NEVER BUMPED INTO EACH OTHER,

Rooster and me, and I never veered from my schedule of hitting his place right after school on Tuesdays and Thursdays when he wasn't home.

That is, until the Thursday when Eli asked if I wanted to help her make bag lunches in the cafeteria after school. Her church group usually made the peanut butter sandwiches for the homeless people on the Lower East Side of Manhattan in the church basement, but the sandwich-making part got canceled that day because the preschool needed the space for a sing-along. I was still five foot eight and she was still five foot ten, but a guy can't say no to an opportunity like making peanut butter sandwiches with Eli, so I basically said yes.

When I got to the cafeteria Eli had a whole assembly line set up on one of the long tables so we could make as many sandwiches as possible in the most efficient way. But I slowed the whole process down on account of the fact that she had to show me how to spread the peanut butter on the bread real thin so those big jars of Jif would last longer, something I was having a really hard time getting a handle on. I acted as if I'd never made a sandwich before since she kept putting her sandwich down and taking my hand in hers and saying, "Do it like this," as the heat rose in my cheeks. But I wasn't about to self-correct. I made forty-seven peanut butter sandwiches that afternoon and each and every one of them started out with way too much peanut butter, and I enjoyed every one of those lessons on how to make those sandwiches probably as much, or more, than the people who got them enjoyed eating them.

But the point was, I showed up late that Thursday afternoon at Rooster's shanty with my cling peaches and chicken-and-stars soup, and he jumped me.

You could say our schedules collided. I'm guessing that he thought I was there to steal his stuff and he had me pegged against a tree before I knew what hit me. Didn't say anything either, just grabbed me and nailed me to a big old oak with his big old grizzly fists like he was gonna kill me.

"Wait," I said, realizing just how much stronger Rooster was than me. "Hold on. I'm just bringing you stuff!" But Rooster had hot eyes, if you know what I mean. Like the crazy people in the scary old movies. Not cold and detached like the serial killer type either, more openly wild and violent—more Jack Nicholson in *One Flew Over the Cuckoo's Nest* than Anthony Hopkins in *The Silence of the Lambs*.

There was a spark of recognition in those eyes, though, just for a split second. So I jumped in to try to see if I could get it to take. I said, "I watch your stuff Wednesday nights at the soup kitchen and Eli gives you cake."

Something registered and Rooster released his grip, just a little. Then I pulled out a can of Campbell's chicken-and-stars soup from my jacket pocket to show him and he let me go a bit more, probably putting two and two together and getting something in the vicinity of four. Not quite four mind you, but close enough. Then Rooster let go altogether, took the can of soup from me, and held up one finger on his right hand like he wanted me to wait and then he stepped into his shanty. I wanted to run, but my feet had a different plan. They just stayed stuck there in the fallen leaves and dirt at the base of that tree like they had set down roots of their own.

When Rooster came back a minute later, he was carrying a dirty white plastic bag all tied up in a knot that looked like it was from a grocery store. Handed it to me like it was a gift. When I took the bag from him I noticed that his gloves were off for the first time since I met him and two of his fingers were missing from his left hand. I just nodded my head and started to inch away, then full on walk off. Then flat-out run. He probably figured that whatever was in that bag made us even. His way of saying, "Thanks for the food and stuff," I supposed.

I didn't dare open the bag until I got home. And then I opened it outside before I went in. Afraid of what I would find. Some rotten food he was saving up for hard times, I figured. Or worse.

I was wrong about the rotten food.

But I was right about the worse.

12

I COULDN'T HAVE GUESSED IT WOULD HAVE BEEN

a gun, though.

Not in a million years.

A .38 caliber Smith & Wesson pistol. With an inlaid wood grip and a six-inch barrel. Wrapped in a rag.

I turned it over in my hands, then looked back in the bag. There were three bullets rattling around loose in the bottom and something else, too.

I dumped it all out and examined the bullets and then ran my fingers over the smooth edges of what was a shiny brass police badge. My hands were shaking when I rewrapped the gun and put it, along with the badge and ammo, back into the bag. Then I hid it in the far corner of my garage. Tucked the bag inside a big stack of broken old bricks my pop had dug up from a walkway that he had replaced a few years back. I walked back to the house, my heart pounding as if I had just run a hundred-yard dash at record-breaking speed. When I stepped inside I found my pop in a heated argument with the TV—the last inning of a Yankee game that, from the sound of it, wasn't going well for the Yankees or for Jackson Higgins. I quickly bent down and patted Lacey, our antique Labrador retriever, on the head, and then walked right through the living room without saying a thing to my pop. I found my mom in the kitchen sitting at the table drinking tea and reading an *Oprah* magazine and she smiled at me when I came in and whispered, "Game's over in ten minutes, then it'll be *All Quiet on the Western Front*."

That was a joke we had 'cause it was the title of a book she loved. I'm not much of a reader but my mom was what I'd call a militant reader and she was always trying to convince us book atheists to come over to the other side—basically meaning me, because Jacey loved books and she had given up on Jackson a long time ago.

I grabbed a plate of food from the fridge, assembling it from all sorts of covered bowls full of leftovers, and without even looking up from Oprah's tips on "How to Have Your Best Summer Ever," my mom said, "I called the school today and spoke to your guidance counselor. Then I signed you up to retake the SATs."

I said, "I told you I'm not taking them again."

And she said, "We'll see."

Then I made a giant glass of chocolate milk and she said, "I hope you're not planning on taking that food upstairs, Joel."

"Please, Mom, just this once. I've got homework to get going on."

Of course, she wasn't really buying into the "just this once" or the homework claim either but she smiled and said, "How about we strike a deal? You take the SATs again this spring and you can eat in your room."

"Just this once? Or for the rest of my life?"

"Not planning on moving out when you graduate from high school are you, Joel?" she teased.

I smiled. "The cooking's too good here, Mom, you know that."

"Well?" she asked.

"What if I say, I'll think about it."

She sat back in her chair and looked me over.

"You'll *think* about taking the SATs?"

I tucked a whole box of cookies under my arm. "That would be a maybe."

"What kind of maybe are we talking about?"

I smiled again. "A *soft* maybe."

"Then *maybe* I'll let you eat upstairs."

I went in for the close. "I'll tuck Jace in."

She grinned. "Joel, I suspect you're playing me."

I said, "You might be right about that," and kissed the top of her head. She just laughed and waved her hand as if dismissing me and I headed up to my room with enough food for a small city as I was thinking about Rooster and all the other homeless people in the US of A that Mrs. T had been telling us about as my mom went back to reading recipes for Georgia sun tea and a stress-free summer. She was just looking for peace and quiet, and I was headed upstairs to google .38 Smith & Wesson revolvers with inlaid wood grips and dead cops and violent crimes in Rockland County.

13

BUT BEFORE I DID THAT GOOGLE SEARCH,

I stuck my head into Jace's room as promised.

He's named Jackson like my pop, but we called him Jace on account of the fact that having two Jacksons was just too confusing. Jace looked like my pop, too. Big and stocky with dark hair and eyes. I looked more like my mom, slight and fair. I didn't mind the blue eyes and fair skin and blond hair, but the *slight* part was real goddamned annoying. Jace was sound asleep, wearing pajamas with trucks on them and feet. My pop kept saying to my mom, "Jesus, Mary"—I don't think I have ever heard my pop say, "Mary" without putting a "Jesus" in front of it—"the kid's too big for damned feet-y pajamas." And he had a point. A few of Jace's toes were sprouting through the plastic bottoms of his pj's like dandelions popping out of the cracks in a sidewalk. But from the look of his room, which was still full of little kids' things like stuffed animals, my mom wasn't ready to give in to "Jace is too big" for anything just yet. Probably figured he'd be too big for *everything* soon enough.

I pulled his covers up and took a toy truck from his hand, then turned out his light. I wondered if he would ever be hungry in his life or if he would be six feet tall someday like Pop. Then I wondered what he would do if he was older and had a gun and a cop's badge stashed away in the back of the garage under the bricks pop had dug up. Right then I was wishing real bad that I had an older brother or a pop who said more than, "Pull the goddamned pitcher." Or, "Jesus, Mary." Or, "What were you doing going and hitting Benj Kutchner? You know that boy ain't right in the head."

I'm not saying Jackson's not a good dad 'cause he is. I know that. I'm just saying my pop's not much of a conversationalist. That is unless that conversation happens to be about gas millage on half-ton pickups or locking differentials or who's offering the best bumper-to-bumper warranty on full-size trucks—or the subway series or left-handed pitchers—and then you'd be in luck.

TEXT FROM JOEL TO ANDY 9:12 p.m.

I called you again and left a message.

I know it's stupid.

But I wish you could call back.

I really need to talk to you right now. I mean really.

TEXT FROM JOEL TO ANDY 9:49 p.m.

I have a gun hidden in my garage. Stuck in between the bricks in the wayback. A homeless guy from the soup kitchen gave it to me. I work at the soup kitchen. On Wednesdays. With Eli.

14

I FOUND NOTHING ON THE INTERNET

that night.

No missing cop.

No dead cop.

No recent gun-related crimes. No armed robbery. No murders.

No nothing.

I kept my search close to home figuring that if Rooster committed an armed robbery or a homicide, he probably did it nearby, being that he didn't have a car and was always pushing that shopping cart with the busted wheel.

And I went back a couple of years, but still came up empty.

By and large the police blotter was populated with shit so ridiculous that you'd think the secretary at the police station would say, "I'm not typing this and I'm not submitting it to the paper either. Tell me about a *real* crime or something that means something instead of this crap!"

If you think that I'm kidding, one entry was that a local shopper called 911 to report a man wearing short shorts near the Pizza Station in town. Next up was a lost purse in the ShopRite parking lot. Then there was this shocker: the Girl Scouts were holding a cookie drive and the troop leader who had dropped the girls off backed into the Hostess cupcake delivery van. That was followed by a report that a raccoon in Mrs. Fillmore's yard on Pine Street that was suspected of being rabid on account of the fact that it was exhibiting unusual behavior of a "particularly aggressive nature" was shot dead in the orchestrated effort of police officers from two towns. And this weekend's capper? A plastic sandwich bag containing a suspicious white powder was found near the entrance to the town swimming pool. The Rockland County hazmat team was brought in to retrieve it and the bag with the white powder was sent to the New York State crime lab, where the suspicious substance was identified as powdered sugar from a donut—I'm guessing of the Dunkin' variety.

Then I read that there were still no suspects—or any new evidence—in the ongoing theft of shopping carts from local stores and I was thinking, *What is going on here and who's in charge?* I mean, there are lots of hungry people in this town and maybe that should be a crime and there's a poor guy living in the woods behind the Richardsons' farm and I have a gun stashed in a stack of old bricks in my garage that was given to me by a man not in control of all his faculties, so maybe the police should adjust their priorities? Then I started thinking that maybe I should become a detective 'cause I had a pretty good handle on where a few of those missing shopping carts were and since every single one of them was full of stuff nobody should be saving in the first place I was wondering why that wasn't something the town could do a bit more about.

But since there was absolutely no mention of stolen guns, or gun violence, or dead police officers or anything else at all remotely important, and since I had no idea why Rooster had given me the gun in the first place, I decided my original guess was right and he probably just figured it was payback for the food and shit. Then I decided to take things under advisement and wait to see what turned up next before settling on what to do about the gun and the rest of the contents of that plastic bag that I had stashed in the back of my garage.

If you're keeping count that was mistake number three in my geometric progression.

TEXT FROM JOEL TO PRINCIPAL REDMAN 12:54 a.m.

If classic Mustangs are too expensive we
could go with Jeep Wranglers.
They're cool.

TEXT FROM JOEL TO PRINCIPAL REDMAN 12:56 a.m.

There are more than two million homeless people in America. Two million. Eli, you know Eli? The girl who fixes everything and makes all the lists? She told me that's more people than live in the entire city of Philadelphia or Houston, or twice as many as who live in Dallas, Texas. We should do something about that.

TEXT FROM JOEL TO PRINCIPAL REDMAN 1:27 a.m.

I have a gun hidden in my garage. A .38 caliber Smith & Wesson revolver. With an inlaid wood grip and a six-inch barrel. In a plastic bag, wrapped in a rag. Behind the bricks.

TEXT FROM JOEL TO PRINCIPAL REDMAN 1:28 a.m.

A homeless guy from the soup kitchen gave it to me.

15

THE NEXT WEDNESDAY

when Rooster showed up at the soup kitchen I waited until Eli brought him his tray of food and then I went over and sat down across from him at the table.

I said, "Hey, how are you doing?" but he kept looking down at his food or over my shoulder at the door like he didn't even hear me. I knew he was probably nervous about his shopping cart, so I said, "Don't worry, I'll go out there to watch your stuff in a minute. I just want to ask you something first."

Rooster was still wearing his heavy winter coat and gloves and hat as he sat there hunched over shoveling big forkfuls of beef stew into his mouth. I leaned in close to him and whispered real low, "What were you doing with a gun? And why'd you give it to me?"

I got nothing back. Rooster just kept eating.

"Do you want me to keep it for you?" I asked as he tackled a big mound of mashed potatoes with gravy.

I couldn't tell if he didn't hear me or didn't understand or just couldn't talk or didn't want to answer, but I kept pushing.

"Are you going to want it back?"

Nothing. He just spread butter on a roll and then moved on to the fruit portion of the meal.

"I mean, I think the gun's cool and everything but I was thinking that maybe I should turn it over to someone. What do you think?"

Still nothing, so I pressed even harder.

"I mean, I don't want to get you in trouble, but if I tell the cops that you . . ."

The mention of cops got his attention real fast and now he was looking up from his food right at me.

Straight in the eyes.

And what I saw on his face scared me.

And not because I was afraid of him or because I thought he was going to hurt someone, but because I saw how scared *he* was.

It was there plain as day in the expression on his face. All around his eyes and mouth was *fear*. Raw and bleeding like an open wound and about as sad a thing as I've ever seen in my whole life. I mean, right there in front of me I saw a kind of hurt that can't be fixed. Everything on his face said *I can't handle any more trouble. I got enough.*

So I doubled back, and leaning in close again so no one else could hear, I said, "I'll keep the gun. No police. No trouble. No nothing. I promise. It's all good."

Rooster's scared look dissolved a bit and then he went back to eating his food. Never said a word, though, but I heard him loud and clear.

I sat there for a bit trying to make sense of what just happened, but once again I came up desert dry and full-on empty, which was something that was happening to me a lot lately.

Then I just stood up and headed outside to stand guard over Rooster's shopping cart while he finished his meal.

TEXT FROM JOEL TO PRINCIPAL REDMAN 12:09 a.m.

That gun I told you about? I decided to keep it.

16

AS MUCH AS I HATED THE SCHOOL BUS,

I hated the cafeteria, too.

The way I figured it, the only difference between the two was that the cafeteria was bigger and served food. At lunch everyone was all clustered together in defined groups, divvied up like there was a median strip separating them. It was like they were all traveling at high speed in lanes going in such opposite directions, and any contact at all between groups, let alone a head-on collision, just might be deadly.

The skinny girls like Angela Marshfield and Brandy Kennedy drinking Diet Coke wearing skinny jeans and skinny tops and too much makeup who would never dream of actually *eating lunch* were heading one way and the ass-saggers with their hats on backward and their pants slipping so low that the crotch was down near their ankles were going another. Then there were the stick-toting, cleat-wearing ass-letes, the skaters, the stoners, and a whole bunch of subcategories and unidentifiables that were not as easy to label, and off to the side on the fringes were the AP Physics wonks headed up by Alex B. Renner in an exclusive group that featured future computer hackers, coders, tech wizards, hedge fund managers, and start-up incubators who were always making some robotic shit out of straws and Bic pens, and for reasons beyond me those projects always seemed to involve lemons. I watched one day as one of them kept running back to get more lemons and more straws from one of the lunch ladies like they were onto something really big. It was the nice lunch lady with the big glasses and the grandma hair named Miss Beverly who was inclined to sneak you an extra cookie or one of those big soft pretzels if you played her just right. She kept smiling at them and giving them lemons like she had a tree growing in the back. They kept typing shit into their cell phone calculators or checking their compasses or maybe they were just sending encrypted text messages back and forth to each other, but whatever they were doing they were having a hell of a good time doing it.

But all that self-selected segregation in the cafeteria didn't flow through to Driver's Ed. I mean, it was like they purposely picked one kid from each of those lanes going in opposite directions and assigned them to the same Driver's Ed car. Like it was some cosmic high school joke.

The consensus was that the Monday, 12:15 p.m. car had the worst collection of misfitted students you could imagine 'cause they put a brand-new kid from Japan named Oshi who didn't speak any English in with Tory Bunson, who was the biggest weed head in the school and should never have been allowed to drive 'cause he had a habit of closing his eyes and napping at inappropriate times and when he walked the halls he was so chill he forgot where he was going half the time. And the two of them were in with Emily Harriman and Brady Stark, who had broken up over the summer and it did not end well. Emily started calling Brady a cheating, body-slamming, misogynistic steak-head meat-stick, and that was only on the days when she felt like being nice. So there was either a stoned weed weasel behind the wheel and a fight going on in the back seat, or a foreign student who couldn't read the road signs and didn't know how to convert miles per hour to kilometers driving and a fight going on in the back seat, or Emily would be driving and crying the whole time and Brady would be in the back with the exchange student and the guy whose future life plans included building a meth lab in his mother's kitchen, or Brady would be driving and pounding the steering wheel 'cause Emily was correct in her assessment that he was basically a steak-head with aggressive tendencies and anger problems and the poor Japanese kid would be stuck in the back with the weed weasel and a sobbing girl.

Here's who I—the future gas station attendant—was sitting next to in the back seat of the white four-door Ford Fiesta starting at 2:15 p.m. on Wednesdays and Fridays and every other Thursday when it wasn't my turn to drive. There was Eli, future bright shining star of something or other; Benj Kutchner, possible parent killer; and Alex B. Renner, future CEO of a global enterprise that would cure malaria or some such shit. He had it all planned out. He was going to be doing an internship at a biotech company in the city this summer, which I only knew 'cause I overheard him tell the guidance counselor, Ms. Emmitt, who I was there to see about my "disappointing performance" on the SATs, that he planned on curing cancer or reinventing the wheel or building a rocket and he was going to get started right away. The way he apparently figured it, there was no point in waiting until he actually knew how to do anything.

Then of course there was Mr. Stanley, the Driver's Ed teacher, with his clipboard and sweaty hands and that left eye that was a bit smaller than his right and twitched real fast when he got nervous. Looked like he was sending secret messages in Morse code to a spy behind enemy lines. He'd be forcefully saying, "Joel, son, you've got to put the car in D for drive not R for reverse and go easy on the gas pedal and try not to lurch out into the roadway with such a heavy foot. Now, try again, and go slowly this time. *Ease* into it." But I was mesmerized by the *di-di-dit dah-dah-dah di-di-dit* of his left eyelid and didn't hear a thing he said until I was back to driving badly and he was yelling again.

"I said, *slowly*! Pull over, son. Now!"

Then I'd lurch the damn Ford Fiesta to the side of the high school parking lot—we hadn't gotten to the actual road yet what with my lead foot and tendency to go in reverse—and Eli would be sitting in the back seat probably wishing she was somewhere else making lists of all the things in the world that needed her attention and Alex B. Renner was memorizing SAT vocab words when he should have been reading the pamphlet Mr. Stanley had handed out on how to drive a motor vehicle 'cause Alex B. Renner couldn't drive for shit, and Benj Kutchner would be bopping to some song he had playing on his phone oblivious to what was going on 'cause he was wearing earbuds that were not allowed but that Mr. Stanley couldn't see because they were running inside his shirt and hidden in his hair and I'd just look at Mr. Stanley and he'd start doing it again. *Di-di-dit dah-dah-dah di-di-dit.*

The funny thing was, 'cause my pop owned a gas station, I'd been driving since I was nine or ten. Could drive circles around old Mr. Stanley. Take the engine of this crap compact car apart, too, and put it back together long before old Stanley could figure out how to pop the hood and check the oil. It's just that Driver's Ed wouldn't have been much fun for any of us if Mr. Stanley knew that. So I kept putting the car in reverse and hitting the gas with a bit too much force and making him work hard to earn his salary. He was getting real frustrated with me as weeks were going by and I wasn't getting the least bit better at driving. I was planning on surprising him on the last day when he gave us the road test, though. Planned on driving textbook perfect then. Needed the certificate for my insurance. Pop said they'd take 247 bucks off my bill if I got it and I'd have to change a lot of flats down at his station to earn that. But the real payoff would be seeing Stanley's left eye going into overdrive with its *dit*s and *dah*s when he figured out that poor worst-in-his-class Joel could actually drive—and probably run the track in a NASCAR race, work the pit with his eyes closed, and cross the finish line first, too.

Besides, I wasn't the only one messing with Mr. Stanley; it was practically a school tradition and a prerequisite to graduate. A couple of times a week the seniors on the football team would either pick the Ford Fiesta up and carry it or jimmy the lock and pop it into neutral and roll it to a new location. Like they'd put it up on a sidewalk or in the back in between the Dumpsters or in the principal's parking space when Redman wasn't there. So poor Stanley would have to wander around the whole campus just to find the car and Principal Redman kept calling him into his office and asking why he was always parking in his spot.

"Why are you doing that?" Benj asked me at the end of the first week when we were standing on the curb waiting for the Driver's Ed car to pull up. "We all know you can drive."

Eli snuck up behind us and said, "He's doing it 'cause he's bored and wants to make a point."

"Which is what?" Benj asked.

"That Joel Higgins doesn't have to follow the rules," Eli answered. "That's all. He's mad at the whole world." And then she ran over to talk to Caitlin Emerson, who just got out of the back seat of Ethan Faukner's black SUV holding a puppy that had a bright red collar and big floppy ears.

Then Alex B. Renner said, "Joel drives like he's a dumb fuck who's a few cans short of a six-pack because he doesn't want Eli to think that she's the worst one."

Benj just looked at him and he was puttin' two and two together and getting way more than four and then I looked right at Alex B. Renner and said, "You're the worst driver. Not Eli. So maybe I'm doing it to make you feel better," and he looked like he wanted to hit me. Then I looked down at the sidewalk thinking about the fact that motorcycles were definitely a way more affordable option for the juniors than Camaros or Jeep Wranglers, figuring Harleys—definitely the Night Rod Specials or Low Riders—would be cool and the best option in my end-the-bus campaign.

Then some other kids wandered over and Benj got down on all fours and started barking like an Afghan hound 'cause Eli and Caitlin were walking over with the puppy on a leash and even though I started thinking about how good Eli would look wearing a leather jacket and straddling a Harley, I hadn't forgotten about what Alex B. Renner said.

Then someone said, "Kutchner just peed all over the sidewalk," and the girls started to scream and then the puppy got scared and peed all over Benj, and I started thinking that even though I didn't know why I was doing what I was doing, Alex B. Renner should have Mrs. Wilson's job because his comment that I was driving like a dumb fuck to make Eli feel better was probably a pretty good assessment.

TEXT FROM JOEL TO ANDY 8:15 p.m.

We're going to get our driver's licenses soon

and everything will be different.

Remember how we would always say that?

Remember?

TEXT FROM JOEL TO ANDY 2:31 a.m.

I learned how to load a gun today.

On YouTube.

17

MR. MORGAN HAD A POLICY

in junior English called "Auto F."

Back on the first day of school he had handed out a packet that was stapled together with a list of all the things that could result in an immediate, non-negotiable, automatic failure on a paper or assignment and everyone was scared to death of him 'cause failing eleventh-grade English meant going to summer school, which was worse than going directly to hell. It was even way worse than working at the gas station, which wasn't really that bad 'cause I got to work on cars and talk shit with the guys and drink soda from the fridge in my pop's office whenever I wanted.

Here are some of the things on Mr. Morgan's list that could get you an Auto F:

Speaking without being called on.
Misspelling any word in Microsoft Word spell check.
Handing in a late assignment.
Egregious misuse of commas.

Potty mouth in class, or in papers.
Dropping pencils.
Unnecessary backpack rummaging.
Smart-aleck comments.
Insulting anyone in class.
Misappropriation of school property.
Not returning a book on time.
Not being prepared for class.
Visible underwear.
Ringing phones.
Text messaging.
Misusing "it's" and "its."
Visible cleavage.
Plumber's crack.
Misusing "they're" and "their" and "there."
Or "who's" and "whose."
Touching other students who don't want to be touched.
Touching other students who do want to be touched.
Dangling modifiers.
Public displays of affection.
Locker sex.
Not indenting paragraphs properly.
Weak or missing thesis statements.
Overuse of ellipses.
Not having good ideas.
Having good ideas and not sharing them.
Eating in class.
Making other people feel bad.

Not having a good attitude.
Not learning anything.
Chewing gum.
Writing on walls with Magic Markers.
Stealing chalk.
Vaping in the bathroom.
Annoying Mr. Morgan.

That's only part of the list because it went on for four more pages but most kids didn't even read it all because it was pretty clear that no one would be passing English this year.

After we left class that day, Benj came up to me and said, "Let's go to Burning Man."

That's how me and Benj officially met.

I said, "First of all, no. And second of all, what is Burning Man?"

He said, "A crazy-assed drug-and-sex fest in the Nevada desert."

"Still no."

"Why not?"

"Because I don't even know you."

Which was true. As I said, Benj was new to CC on account of the fact that he had to live with his aunt because he might have killed his parents. He just looked at me that day like what difference did it make that he didn't know me, what with the fact that he didn't know anyone, what with him being brand-new and this being the first day of school.

"Why do you want to go to a drug-and-sex fest in the desert with *me*?"

"Because I don't know anyone else and it's in the summer and it's crazy fun and I'm going to be feeling bad."

"Why are you going to be feeling bad?"

"Because I'm going to fail eleventh-grade English."

He had a point.

Then Eli and Alex B. Renner walked over and I was about to say, "This is Benj, he's new," when Kutchner said, "They have an orgy tent and a speed boner contest."

We all just looked at him 'cause that was not the best way to introduce yourself at a new school. After that comment I decided that a formal introduction was no longer necessary.

Then Benj said, "I'd definitely win the speed boner contest."

And Alex B. Renner looked at him with a sneer on his face and said, "Everyone has to be good at something," and walked away. And then Eli smiled nicely at Benj because she was always so polite, and then she invited Benj to her church group.

Neither me nor Kutchner had a response to that.

I mean, after what he just said?

Come on, we had absolutely nothing.

TEXT FROM JOEL TO ANDY 1:27 a.m.

My mom got new controllers. She said she wouldn't until she figured out who smashed them but Jacey cried and held his breath, so they went to Target.

TEXT FROM JOEL TO PRINCIPAL REDMAN 1:43 a.m.

And one more thing. Here are some words Mr. Morgan gave us to study for the SAT. I bet you don't know what any of them mean and I bet you've had a perfectly good life even though you don't.

Abjur—to renounce solemnly
Acerbic—biting, sarcastic
Inchoate—not fully formed
Inimical—being hostile to

They are all grandiloquent—that means pompous, bombastic, overly colorful words. Here's another one they should ditch: loquacious. And this one too: pedantic. More words no one will ever use.

TEXT FROM JOEL TO PRINCIPAL REDMAN 2:32 a.m.

Maybe retire Andy's gym locker too. It's 127B in the boys' locker room. The one with the World of Warcraft sticker on the front.

TEXT FROM JOEL TO ANDY 3:10 a.m.

If you were here and you liked the new kid who maybe killed his parents we could let him sit with us at lunch. Or maybe not. Whatever you would want is cool.

TEXT FROM JOEL TO ANDY 3:17 a.m.

I have a few new diseases to go along with the insomnia, parasite, phlebitis, pulmonary embolism, and everything else I have. I won't get into the details, but just so you know.

TEXT FROM JOEL TO PRINCIPAL REDMAN 3:32 a.m.

That gun I told you about? I still have it.
And the guy who gave it to me?
There's something wrong with him and
someone should try to help him.
I mean, someone besides me.

18

I SAW THIS MOVIE ONCE WITH WILL SMITH IN IT,

and in the movie he used to have a good job but some stuff happened and he lost everything and he ended up homeless and he was a single father who had to sleep in the subway with his son who was five years old like Jace.

The actor who played his kid was Will Smith's real son, Jaden, which had to be cool, I mean, to be a little kid like that and be so rich and famous and get to make a movie with your dad. I mean, come on.

But anyway, in the movie, Will Smith was down on his luck but he was *freakin' Will Smith*, so you knew that he would rebound and get a good job, and by the end of the movie he did, but it broke your heart to see how hard he was trying to protect his kid and make him happy and get him food and make sure that he had a place to sleep. The movie version of homeless Will Smith was trying so hard to pretend that everything *was* okay even when it wasn't okay and you would never believe it ever would be okay but in the end it was okay because movies like this tend to end well if they star Will Smith even though in real life it didn't usually work out that way. But when I was watching the film, all I could think about was that the real Will Smith and his real son lived in a mansion with a tennis court and they had shopping bags full of cash and a chauffer and a chef and maybe a masseuse and a butler and even though he was homeless in this movie, come on, it's fucking Will Smith with his real kid and Will Smith is too smart and too well dressed and too well spoken to be homeless ever, even in a made-up movie. Especially because movie homeless Will Smith slept in the subway bathroom wearing a business suit and still looked good, so I thought it was all just Hollywood bullshit.

And then I met the Hendricks Street soup kitchen Will Smith.

He came in through the door and he could have been the president of IBM or your dentist or your dad or Will Smith except for the fact that he was white. When I saw him I was expecting that he was going to ask for Mrs. T 'cause he wanted to make a sizable donation or build people houses or maybe he was going to say that he owned the building and was going to shut down this place because Old Navy could pay more rent, but then he got in line and took a plate.

Me and Eli served him meat loaf with green beans and gravy and Eli said, "Sorry, sir, but there is no cake tonight," and Hendricks Street Will Smith smiled at her real nice and said, "That's okay, sweetheart." He then picked up his tray and started to walk away but turned back and said, "What's your name?" And she smiled and said, "Eli." And Hendricks Street Will Smith said, "Let me guess. Your dad named you after Eli Manning? The quarterback for the Giants?"

Eli said, "No, sir, my parents named me after Eli in the Bible, the high priest of Shiloh," and Hendricks Street Will Smith just nodded his head probably thinking, *That sucks. It would be way more fun to be named after Eli Manning than some dude from the Bible.*

When he sat down to eat I said, "You're not even old enough to be named after Eli Manning and we should call him Will Smith."

But Eli said, "We shouldn't because he has a real name and he talks to us and he'll probably tell us his name the next time he comes here."

But I said, "He didn't say his name this time and I want to call him Will Smith."

And Eli said, "Don't get in a huff, Joel." And then she added, "Wait, isn't Will Smith black?"

I said, "Of course Will Smith is black. Haven't you ever seen *The Fresh Prince of Bel-Air* or *Men in Black—Protecting the Earth from the Scum of the Universe*?"

And she said, "No. Is that even a real movie title?"

And I said, "Eli, you have to stop going to church and making lists so much and start watching a lot more TV and going to the movies."

And she said, "Oh, Joel, you are too cute."

I told her *Too Cute* was a TV show about puppies and kittens that Jacey watched all the time with Jesus, Mary and then Eli kissed my cheek and I almost burst into flames.

I mean, *really almost burst into flames*.

If Eli's God was watching He—or She—would have scooped me up right then and there and ended my life with a bolt of lightning, saying, "It's over, Joel. You've had too much happiness for one person already."

Eli had that effect on me. She was like cake with sprinkles.

TEXT FROM JOEL TO PRINCIPAL REDMAN 3:11 a.m.

That gun I told you about?

Sometimes I take it out and put a bullet in and think about how one little thing can change everything.

19

"IF YOU THINK A SOUP KITCHEN'S NOT IN YOUR FUTURE,

maybe think again.

"Forty-one point two million people in America are food insecure." That's what Mrs. T told us. Not to scare us, mind you, just 'cause part of what she was supposed to do in exchange for our volunteering was teach us some stuff. When she said it, Eli was looking at her phone and she leaned over to me and said, "Forty-one point two million's larger than the population of Canada, Peru, or Poland." Then she added, "Or Venezuela, Morocco, Sudan, or North Korea," before I even figured out what she was talking about because all I could think about when she said that was how good she smelled.

Like vanilla and sweet cherries.

With a hint of coconut.

"How do you know that?" I asked on the north side of an inhale. "I mean, all those population numbers?" And Eli said, "I have a thing for numbers."

I said, "No, you don't, Eli. You have a thing for cake."

"And pi," she said.

"As in, apple or blueberry?" I asked.

"As in 3.14159," she replied.

"So you googled pi?"

"No, I googled countries with less than forty-one point two million in population."

Then Mrs. T started up again. "What does it mean to be food insecure? Anyone?"

She looked at the sea of blank faces and then she answered herself since there was no one in this group who would have had a clue. Benj Kutchner was lucky if he could spell his own name correctly two consecutive times in a row and he was preoccupied at that moment, scraping something nasty off the sole of his right sneaker with a fork. Amanda, one grade up from us at CC, was texting and making calls on her cell phone, and from what I could tell she was way more interested in getting her nails done than feeding anyone. Then there were Marjorie and Macy, older women who stayed to themselves and did most of the cooking, who were furiously knitting what looked like matching dog sweaters, and neither of them piped in with an answer either. And Eli would normally be sitting there paying close attention but she was too busy to answer because she was googling global stats on world hunger on her phone and typing out one of her lists.

"It means that you don't always know where your next meal is coming from," Mrs. T finally said as Eli continued identifying entire countries with populations less than the number of hungry people in America. *Iraq, Saudi Arabia, Algeria* . . . Mrs. T kept talking, and I kept looking at her like I was real interested even though no one else even bothered to fake it. Then she just waved her hand and said, "Get out of here. We have food to serve to the hungry," but I couldn't help but feel that despite our good intentions, we were just shuffling the cards in the losing deck of life for a group already dealt a bad hand, some of whom had started out a few cards short to boot.

I mean, I was trying real hard but kept coming up empty.

That is, in the how-to-put-a-good-spin-on-what-we-were-doing department.

TEXT FROM JOEL TO PRINCIPAL REDMAN 10:09 p.m.

We really should plant food for the hungry.

I was thinking we could plow up the teachers'

parking lot and plant vegetables.

I mean, come on, the teachers don't have to drive.

TEXT FROM JOEL TO ANDY 10:47 p.m.

Homework sucks. This is what I'm supposed to be working on:

If $3x - y = 12$ what is the value of $8x/2y$?

A. 2^{12}

B. 4^4

C. 8^2

D. The value cannot be determined from the information given.

There is no way I will ever be able to answer that question.

So I'm playing NBA 2K18 instead.

The simulated NBA Finals match between the Golden

State Warriors and Cleveland Cavaliers.

TEXT FROM JOEL TO ELI 2:27 a.m.

Mrs. Wilson, the school psychologist, said that making so many lists could just mean that someone is super organized but it might be OCD. I don't want to scare you but I looked it up. That means obsessive-compulsive disorder.
Mrs. Wilson said that making lists might give the person a sense of calm when they are worried they might forget stuff or it could be a form of mental illness.

Either way she's not sure.

I was thinking that since your lists have such big things on them, then maybe they give you a feeling of structure in a messy world. I was thinking that we should probably just clean up the messy world. That way you wouldn't have to make lists.

Or you could make lists. Either way, I'm good with both.

TEXT FROM JOEL TO ELI 2:43 a.m.

I didn't tell Mrs. Wilson that you make lists. I said I was asking for a friend so she basically thinks that it's me. I saw her writing in my file. She probably wrote here's one more thing wrong with Joel. Now he's making lists. He's a mess. And unfixable.

TEXT FROM JOEL TO ELI 2:54 a.m.

I didn't mean you were a mess and unfixable because you're perfect. I meant me. I'm a mess.

TEXT FROM JOEL TO ELI 3:15 a.m.

Don't feel bad. I'm probably wrong about the whole OCD thing. I think everyone has something bad wrong with them. I told my mom she has tuberculosis and my dad has mesothelioma and Jacey has Rocky Mountain spotted fever. And that's just this week.

My mom says she's perfectly healthy and so is my dad and Jacey just has eczema, but she's basically wrong. I googled it.

TEXT FROM JOEL TO ELI 3:22 a.m.

I tried making a list of everything that I needed to do. It didn't fix anything or help my bad thoughts. But you should still do it. If it makes you feel better.

TEXT FROM JOEL TO ELI 3:46 a.m.

If you want to see Mrs. Wilson I could go with you. Either way. I'm okay with going or not going.

TEXT FROM JOEL TO ELI 3:51 a.m.

I have a gun in my garage. Sometimes when I feel bad I take it out and think about what would happen if I pulled the trigger. It doesn't make me feel any better, but I still do it.

THE NEXT DAY ELI WALKED OVER TO ME

when I was standing at my locker and said, "Joel, do you want to come with me to my church group after school today?"

"Will God be there?" I asked as I looked at her. "Like actually show up?"

Eli leaned back against the lockers and sighed. "Since God is everywhere, yes, He—or She—will be at my church group."

"If He—or She—is everywhere then He—or She—is here, too," I said. "So that means there's no point in actually going to your church group."

Eli looked at me and I could tell that she was frustrated. "Are you going to keep doing this?"

"Doing what?"

"Being really annoying and acting like you don't want to come."

"Probably. Plus I'm not acting. I don't believe in God. And you know why."

I slammed my locker shut. I knew Eli wasn't asking me on a date. She was always asking everyone to go to church group with her and she was just trying to make me feel better. I was pretty much something that was broken and needed to be fixed and she was a fixer.

"So you're not coming with me, then?" she asked.

"I didn't say that."

"So you are, then?" Eli was starting to look pissed off. I decided I better stop.

"After school today, right?"

"Yes, and we can take the bus."

"It would be better if I drove us in my Camaro."

"Joel, you don't have a Camaro. Or a driver's license."

"I might soon."

"But not by three fifteen today."

"No. Not by three fifteen today."

"So you'll meet me by the buses?"

"I'll meet you by the buses."

"Just so you know, Benj is coming, too."

"What? No. How come?"

"Because I asked him to."

"That proves it, then."

"Proves what?"

"That there is no God."

"Joel!"

"If there was a God, there wouldn't be forty-one point two million hungry people in America and Benj would not be coming with us to your church group." I was going to add something else but ReThought and stopped myself.

"Joel, that's not how it works. God does not work solely on your behalf."

"That, Eli, is the crux of the whole problem with Him—or Her."

When I said that, Eli went from annoyed and pissed off to slightly amused. And then she laughed. I wanted to kiss her right then, I really did.

Almost did, actually.

But then Alex B. Renner walked by and slapped me on the back and said, "Go for it, Higgins, what's the worst that could happen?" And I turned bright red and just walked away.

Two hours later when I got to the front of the school where the buses lined up, Eli was waiting on the sidewalk with Benj. When I walked over he said, "Burning Man is in a hundred and thirty-three days," and Eli said, "If we can make seven hundred sandwiches, seven hundred people won't be hungry tonight." Then Eli, who was now looking at her phone, said, "In the US, 35,092 people die in car crashes each year. That's 96.14 a day," and Benj said, "That's 4.006 people dying every hour," and I said, "How did you know that? And you can't have .006 of a person." Then Eli said, "We should all say a prayer for the 4.006 people who just died," and I said, "No fucking way, I don't believe in God." Just without the "fucking" part and without the "no" part and without the "God" part, which basically means that I said, "That sounds like a lovely idea," but then the bus we were supposed to take pulled up and none of us had time to pray because we had to get on fast if we wanted a seat.

Everyone at the church group except Eli basically sucked.

The leader was this skinny, weaselly, wimpy guy who had a runny nose and the pale blue, almost white, glow-in-the-dark eyes of an alien and he shook your hand too long if you were new to the group like he thought love and healing were flowing out of his fingertips, or if he held on to you long enough he could suck out any ungodly marrow or maybe transport you to the mother ship and harvest your organs. The way I figured it, he was probably not a priest or minister but more like a brother or a monk or maybe an extraterrestrial emissary sent by a higher power to foster the spiritual evolution of young earthlings. Either that or maybe he was a child molester who was hired to lead the church group and drive the van with the sandwiches into the city.

That basically sums up Ted.

And, in a nutshell, the kids in the group were all pretty much whiney, sniveling, ass-kissing do-gooders, too.

Okay, that's not true at all. They were all nice.

Much nicer than me.

Even Ted, the church group leader and van driver who may have been a priest or minister or a monk but probably not an alien, child-molesting space brother was pretty nice.

They were all helping people because they believed in God and service and I pretty much thought the world sucked and I didn't believe in anything good. I mean, come on, it's pretty hard to have a positive attitude with so much bad shit going on around us. I guess I just had a different perspective than they did, and sometimes I knew I was wrong, but mostly not, mainly because sometimes even when you're doing and thinking something even if it's wrong it can feel right to you at the time—and comfortable. But to me church group was just one of those weird, incomprehensible things in the universe like french fries without ketchup, meatless Mondays, and cold fusion.

On a positive note, there was no praying or church mumbo jumbo and luckily Benj was really good at making sandwiches. I mean, he got the whole peanut-butter-spreading thing right off the bat, which was good because I had been hoping Eli would continue to be my private peanut butter tutor for life. Then, just as I tempted her to come running over by fabricating a peanut butter emergency—by putting almost half a jar of Jif on a single piece of bread—she got distracted because some girl named Becky with red hair and freckles who was not from our school said that we shouldn't be putting jelly on the sandwiches because jelly has too much sugar and sugar causes diabetes and heart disease and Eli said maybe jelly is nice when you are hungry and have no food and besides it tastes good and Becky said we're killing people with these sandwiches and she went all middle school on us and started to cry and then Ted, the priest or minister or brother or monk or alien child molester with glow-in-the-dark irises and marrow-sucking tentacle hands, had to take Becky outside to calm her down.

So now I had to not only make sure that I spread the peanut butter thinly, but I also had to make sure to spread the jelly real thin because I didn't want to kill anyone. Then Eli took out her phone and I said, "What are you doing?" as I basically scraped two pounds of peanut butter off of a single slice of bread and put it back in the jar myself because she was unavailable to assist me and she said, "Googling sugar in jelly," and Benj said, "Oh no, here we go." Then Eli said, "Becky's right, there's a ton of sugar in jelly. Three tablespoons of jelly has the same amount of sugar as a twelve-ounce soda, which is almost ten teaspoons." And then *she* looked like she was going to cry. Then the whole church group got upset because no one knew what to do because basically we were giving diabetes and heart disease to the homeless people in New York City.

And that sucked.

Plus as one kid pointed out, God probably wouldn't be happy with that, which sent everyone into a tailspin.

So we sat in a circle and sang "Kumbaya."

Clearly God didn't show up.

Not even for a minute.

The way I figured it, He—or She—was probably just too busy planning earthquakes and plagues and giving kids cancer to be worried about grape jelly and homeless people getting diabetes.

That pretty much summed up church group. I mean, it could not have gone any worse.

21

"WHY DO WE HAVE TO READ

all these gay books?"

That's what Benj Kutchner asked Mr. Morgan, our English teacher, the day after the jelly incident in the church basement, but not until after he followed proper protocol and raised his hand and got called on, on account of the Auto F policy.

Mr. Morgan asked, "What makes you say they're gay books?" and Benj looked like he had just asked him why he wasn't wearing pants and then everyone in the entire class began looking at Benj like he wasn't wearing pants 'cause nobody would have made the gay book comment even though most of us were thinking about it because every single book we read this year had some gay people in it, so it seemed like it was the overarching theme for eleventh-grade English that nobody happened to bring up. Like Mr. Morgan had decided that we should hurry up and read all the gay books ever written but not mention it to us so it was like there was a big gay elephant in the classroom that nobody would bring up. And then Benj became all unglued 'cause he wasn't expecting that response from Mr. Morgan and he said, "Um, I don't know, but it seems that . . ."

Then Benj looked at the floor like he was really interested in the pattern of scratches where the desk chair had dug into the linoleum and said, "I mean, it's just that in the last book we read there was the . . ." and his sentence just trailed off probably because he didn't want to actually say what the "the" was. And then he said, "Well, and then in the book before that, there were the two girls who . . ."

He was digging a hole so fast and for some reason he wasn't smart enough to stop.

A couple of guys in the back of the classroom made a noise probably because they were thinking about "the two girls who . . ." but then Benj kept digging himself deeper like he was oblivious to where he was headed, adding ". . . well, it's just that I was wondering if, I mean, why we are reading books that . . ."

Holy shit. He was dying and Mr. Morgan just let him struggle along. You could hear a pin drop in the classroom but there were some kids making noise out in the hall, so Mr. Morgan walked over and closed the door. Then Kutchner began bumbling even more on account of the fact that he was probably now worried that the books we were reading weren't even gay books in the first place or that nobody else noticed anything gay about them and he was probably just reading too much into things or maybe he read too fast and got it wrong and maybe he should go back and reread them and now he made things way worse for himself 'cause he was the new kid who nobody liked and now he would be known as the new kid who thinks regular books are gay books. And that's the kind of thing that's hard to recover from.

"Who else thinks we are reading gay books?"

A few hands started to go up slowly and then more followed. *A lot more.*

Which made me feel better about the other kids 'cause it was like throwing a lifeline to the new kid who basically everyone hated. I mean, they didn't really *hate him*, it's just that they didn't really *notice him either*. And when they did he usually just said something off or weird or Kutchner-like and someone would roll their eyes and someone else would make a face and walk away and then it would be all awkward 'cause no one who was left wanted to be there and then someone else would do something stupid like kick a locker and someone else would laugh and then a girl would walk by and we would all pretty much forget about Benj and whatever stupid thing he said.

Then Mr. Morgan asked, "What makes something 'a gay book'?" as he looked around the classroom and then called on Steven Watts, who always had his hand up even when he had no clue what the answer was.

"If there are gay characters?" he asked and a whole bunch of heads nodded in agreement.

"So by that formula, if there's a female character in a book then it's a 'women's book'? Or if there's a Chinese character it's a 'Chinese book'? Or if there's a heterosexual couple it's a 'straight book'?"

Everyone just looked confused.

"More than half of you had your hands up when I asked if you thought that these books we are reading are 'gay books,' yet every one of these books is *really* about something else, like self-identity or self-harm or romance or suicide or bullying or abuse."

Nobody moved or talked.

"They're not *gay books,* Mr. Kutchner. They're just *books.*"

More silence. The kind that makes it uncomfortable to breathe.

"But perhaps a better question is, why do you *think* they are gay books?"

Eli put her hand up and Mr. Morgan called on her.

"Because we've read hundreds of books and very few, if any, of them have had gay characters in them. So maybe when we read about a gay character it jumps out at us as a gay book?"

"Great, Eli. So perhaps what Mr. Kutchner really meant to ask was, *Why are we reading so many books with gay characters in them this year?* Does anyone want to take a shot at answering that question?"

Mr. Morgan looked around the classroom and everyone had their eyes riveted on him but no hands went up.

"It's really simple. It's because *we can.*"

He looked around at us slowly. Almost one by one as if he was memorizing our faces but no one said anything probably because we were all just thinking about what he said and then I started wondering if Kutchner was gay or if Mr. Morgan was gay or if the other kids thought I was gay and I was busy thinking about who was gay and who wasn't until I heard Mr. Morgan say, "Anyone want to know why this is particularly important?"

Nobody put a hand up.

"The reason that it's so important that you read these books is because you and I are lucky enough to live in a country—and a school district—where we *can* read books with gay themes and gay characters and that's not true today in most of the world."

Mr. Morgan turned around and started writing some names of countries on the blackboard:

Syria, Russia

Then he turned back to face the class and said, "Do you know what would happen in these countries if you got caught reading any of the books we've read this year?"

No one raised a hand this time either.

"You could be arrested and put to death."

He picked up the book we were reading from his desk, "Just for reading this book." He picked up the last book we had read. "Or this one." Then another. "Or this one."

Then Mr. Morgan turned around and started erasing the blackboard and Eli leaned over to me and said, "There are a lot more countries than that where you could get killed or put in prison for reading a book with a gay or lesbian or transgender or bigender or gender fluid or any sexually dissident character." Then she started reading from her phone, whispering,

"Algeria
Angola
Botswana
Burundi . . ."

I whispered back, "Stand up and read them to the class."

"I'll get an Auto F."

"So what?"

". . . Cameroon
Comoros

Egypt
Eritrea . . ."

I called out, "Eli has something to say."

Mr. Morgan turned around and didn't yell at me or give me an Auto F for not raising my hand and Eli slowly stood up and she still had her phone out, which would qualify for an Auto F, too, and she started reading the list of countries where you could be arrested or get the death penalty for reading a book with a gay character.

". . . Ethiopia, Gambia, Ghana, Guinea, Kenya . . ."

Then Mr. Morgan turned and started scrawling them on the blackboard as she spoke.

". . . Liberia
Libya
Malawi
Mauritania
Mauritius
Morocco
Namibia
Nigeria
Senegal
Sierra Leone
Somalia
South Sudan
Sudan

Swaziland
Tanzania
Togo
Tunisia
Uganda
Zambia
Zimbabwe
Afghanistan
Bangladesh
Bhutan
Brunei
Daesh
India
Iran
Iraq
Kuwait
Lebanon
Malaysia
Maldives
Myanmar
Oman
Pakistan
Palestine/Gaza Strip
Qatar
Saudi Arabia
Singapore
Sri Lanka
Syria

Turkmenistan
United Arab Emirates
Uzbekistan
Yemen
Antigua & Barbuda
Barbados
Dominica
Grenada
Guyana
Jamaica
St. Kitts & Nevis
St. Lucia
St. Vincent & the Grenadines
Trinidad & Tobago
Cook Islands
Indonesia
Kirbati
Papua New Guinea
Samoa
Solomon Islands
Tonga
Tuvalu
Russia
Lithuania
Ukraine
Moldova
Belarus
Kyrgyzstan."

It took Eli a long time to get through the list because there were eighty-two countries and Mr. Morgan had to tell her to slow down because he couldn't write that fast and when she was finished everyone got quiet but then Benj raised his hand and when he got called on he said, "Eli, you made your point seventy-two countries ago."

Then Alex B. Renner raised his hand and got called on and he said, "Daesh doesn't count because it's just another acronym for ISIS and really isn't an actual country, so it's really eighty-one countries," and then Benj said, "If you say 'Daesh' then ISIS says they will cut out your tongue," and then Andrew Kline said, "Well, that's ironic because we're talking about free speech," and I was thinking that Mr. Morgan is really inconsistent with the whole Auto F thing and that I didn't get to see Eli enough because we only saw each other in English and on the bus and in Driver's Ed and in the hallway by our lockers and at lunch and after Gym sometimes unless it was Wednesday and then I got to see her at the soup kitchen. Everyone else was quiet on account of the gay book thing and the Auto F thing and nobody was texting or whispering or dropping pencils on the floor or riffling through backpacks unnecessarily or using apostrophes inappropriately or dangling modifiers either.

When Eli finished Mr. Morgan erased some of the countries 'cause there was no more room to write on the blackboard and he wrote this instead:

Winnie-the-Pooh was banned in schools in Kansas.

Then he turned around and said, "Does anyone know why?"

He pointed at Andrew Kline, who had his hand up again.

"Because Winnie-the-Pooh is gay?"

"No. Anyone else?"

Nobody raised a hand.

"Because some people think that it's an insult to God if animals are . . ." And Mr. Morgan turned his back and the chalk was squeaking on the blackboard,

anthropomorphized

Then he turned back around and added, ". . . which means given human qualities or emotions. In this case, the book was banned in a part of the country we live in because the animals in *Winnie-the-Pooh* talk."

Nobody said anything. It was as quiet as the time in seventh grade when Kenny Holmes asked the health teacher if our parents have sex and he said, "Yes, I suspect that they do. All the time, actually."

Then Mr. Morgan said, "And *Winnie-the-Pooh* was also banned in Poland because . . . ?"

Benj's hand went up and Mr. Morgan called on him.

"Mr. Kutchner?"

"Because it's an insult to God if animals talk?"

"No. Anyone else?"

No hands went up.

"Because in the book Pooh isn't wearing pants—"

What the . . . ?

"—and Pooh is not clearly identified as either male or female and some people in Poland perceived that to mean that Winnie-the-Pooh is . . ."

Mr. Morgan turned and the chalk was squeaking again . . .

intersex

"Which, for those of you who don't know . . ."

Now, in a normal class there would have been all sorts of snickers and comments thrown out, but under the threat of an Auto F it was completely silent.

". . . means having a condition that often includes ambiguous sexual organs and atypical sex characteristics."

Okay, now there were a few snorts from the back of the room 'cause teachers usually didn't say "sexual organs" but nobody actually said any real words and it would be hard to tell where the snickers came from because there were so many, so Mr. Morgan ignored them.

Then it got real quiet again because everyone was probably thinking about whether Winnie-the-Pooh was a boy or a girl and whether he or she should be wearing boxers or briefs or boxer briefs or pink panties with ribbons or if bears should wear underpants *ever* and about all the other books with naked bears and how we never thought about them as *being naked* and I was trying to remember if the Berenstain Bears were naked in those books or if they wore clothes because I couldn't remember because I hadn't seen those books or thought about Brother or Sister Bear in so long and then I started thinking that sometimes a bear with no pants is just because bears don't wear pants especially real bears and teddy bears and people who read *Winnie-the-Pooh* aren't ever thinking about sex or bear sex or underpants because they just aren't.

And then Mr. Morgan called on Benj, who said, "There was a bear named Pedals in New Jersey that walked standing up like a man."

Every single kid in the class probably wanted to ask him if Pedals wore underwear or if you could see his junk or if he talked like a human but some of us like me decided that could lead to an Auto F, so we didn't.

I was pretty sure snarky remarks were on the Auto F list.

But Mr. Morgan just ignored the Pedals-the-bear comment

completely and kept teaching. I noticed that teachers tended to do that when Benj blurted out weird stuff and non sequiturs. They tell you to do that with little kids or dogs. *Just reward the good behavior and ignore the bad behavior and hope that it goes away.* Jesus, Mary did that with Jace when he started saying curse words and she did it with Lacey, who has a bladder problem and basically pees on the floor all the time. My mom said you can extinguish the bad behavior by not giving it any attention.

I don't think it worked very well 'cause Jacey still drops the f-bomb and Lacey is going to get the world record for number of times a dog's peed inside the house. Jackson keeps saying, "We should fuckin' wash Jacey's mouth out with soap and should smack Lacey with a rolled-up newspaper," but every time he says that, Jesus, Mary just smacks Jackson with a rolled-up newspaper and tells him that's "not a Christian thing to do."

Then Mr. Morgan said that *Winnie-the-Pooh* was also banned in a number of Muslim countries because some people perceived Piglet to be an insult to Allah.

I wanted to ask, "Is that because of the pork thing?" And I really wanted to know because I knew that Muslims didn't eat pork but I couldn't think of any other reason why Piglet would be insulting to Allah but I ReThought and didn't dare ask in case that question was insulting to Muslims if we had any Muslims in the class, which I didn't think we did but you never know. Plus it was possible that asking weird questions was on the Auto F list, which I hadn't memorized due to its length, and that just because he let Benj and me and Eli off the hook once today for an Auto F violation it didn't mean that we could get away with it again and what with the fact that Benj had a long history of asking weird questions he might be a special case anyway. I mean, there was no way to tell if Mr. Morgan would let me off the hook if I asked about Piglet and pork.

Mr. Morgan kept talking but I texted my mom even though if I got caught texting it was an Auto F.

I typed, *Muslims don't eat pork right?*

She typed, *????????????*

I typed, *Do we have the Winnie-the-Pooh book at home?*

She texted, *Yes.*

I typed, *Can I read it to Jace tonight?*

She typed, *Of course. Y? U don't like to read.*

I wrote, *Because maybe I do like to read.*

She wrote, *???????*

Then I typed, *And animals should be able to talk and bears don't wear pants and Piglet is cute and never insulted anyone's God and because I can read gay books if I want to.*

She texted, *R U OK?*

I texted, *Yes*, and put a smiley face and a pig emoji after it.

She texted, *Is Winnie-the-Pooh gay???*

I typed, *It doesn't matter if he's gay or not.*

There was a long wait and then she typed, *Joel, are you trying to tell me that you are gay?*

I typed, *NO, I AM JUST TRYING TO UNDERSTAND THE WHOLE BEAR THING.*

She typed back, *I HAVE NO IDEA WHAT YOU ARE TALKING ABOUT.*

She used all caps sometimes even when she wasn't even mad.

I did, too.

I typed, *IK.*

She typed, *WHAT ARE YOU DOING, JOEL?*

I thought about typing, *Figuring shit out or learning about free speech and banned books or GROWING UP,* but just typed, *Nothing.*

Then I snuck my phone back into the pouch in my sweatshirt and Mark Kleinman, future district attorney of Rockland County, said, "So, Mr. Morgan, based on everything you just told us I would say that you are a staunch believer in free speech."

But Mr. Morgan was no fool and he knew where Kleinman was headed, so he said, "Yes, Mr. Kleinman, I am. Very much so. Just not in this classroom."

And there was a snicker from the back of the room but Mr. Morgan didn't lob the Auto F bomb for it. He just waved his hand and said, "Get out of here, all of you. Oh, and one more thing. Who knows what vacation is coming up at the end of May?"

Stevie Williams yelled out, "Huzzah! A day off from school!"

Kutchner said, "He should get an Auto F."

Mr. Morgan said, "It's Memorial Day. And the veterans we will be honoring gave their lives fighting for your right to read these books. They've been fighting to defend freedom and our First Amendment right to free speech—and the freedoms of others around the world, as well—since our country was born. Remember that next month as you eat hamburgers and rot your brains playing video games and as you read the first hundred pages of the next book on your reading list this weekend that would be outlawed in many countries. We'll be discussing it on Monday."

It got real quiet.

There were still six minutes left in class, but nobody left the room. Pretty much we just sat there thinking about stuff.

I was thinking about banned books and free speech and veterans.

And the soup kitchen.

And Rooster.

And Spindini.

And Eli.

And how hot she looked right now.

And how big the world was.

And how it sucked that I was still short.

And that the world is unfair.

But mostly I was thinking about what an idiot I was and how all of this tied together to make one big fucking colossal mess.

TEXT FROM JOEL TO PRINCIPAL REDMAN 1:12 a.m.

Mr. Morgan should get a raise. He is the only good teacher I have ever had. Except for Miss Ellison in first grade. She was nice too.

TEXT FROM JOEL TO ANDY 1:29 a.m.

If you were gay I would be cool with that.

I'm not saying that I think you're gay, I'm just saying it would be okay if you were.

Not that it matters what I think, but still.

Either way, straight or gay.

Or not gay and not straight.

Pretty much anything is good.

22

THE NEXT TIME I DROPPED THINGS OFF

for Rooster I brought him a towel and soap and a blanket and some other stuff and a book that used to be Andy's favorite.

The whole point of the book was that basically life can be hard but it can be awesome, too, so hang in there.

I mean, I didn't read it or anything. I only knew that because Andy told me.

I wrote Rooster a note on sticky paper and basically said I don't know if you like to read but I figured you might. And don't worry that it's a kids' book, it's fun. Then I wrote something to the effect that I was thinking that maybe a fun book would help him forget about things. I stuck the note right onto the front cover and put the book next to a can of ravioli and three packages of pudding cups and six boxes of Girl Scout cookies and a blanket and then just left.

The next day, Jesus, Mary looked really annoyed when I got home from school and she said, "This is getting ridiculous, Joel. Everything is disappearing. Who ate all the Girl Scout cookies?"

I said, "Don't look at me, I didn't have any. Not even one. It was probably Jacey."

I'm pretty sure she didn't buy it.

Then I said, "I like to read now," mainly to change the subject.

She smiled and said, "That's really, really great, Joel! What are you interested in reading? I mean, what type of books?"

I said, "Pretty much the ones that are banned."

Jesus, Mary looked at me real hard for a minute and then she said, "Interesting. So you're a rebel reader."

I said, "I guess that makes sense if you think about it," and she laughed.

My mom just kept standing there looking at me without saying anything and it seemed like she was really happy. Or maybe just surprised.

Either that or she was just staring at me hoping I would crack and confess about the Girl Scout cookies and the socks and all the other stuff that was apparently just walking out of here on its own.

It was probably the cookie-and-sock thing, not the Joel-made-me-happy thing.

I mean, come on. It's me. I pretty much don't make anyone happy.

The next day after school I found three books from the library on my bed with a sticky note on the front listing all the places they were banned.

The Outsiders by S. E. Hinton.

The Catcher in the Rye by J. D. Salinger.

And *Beloved* by Toni Morrison.

I picked them up and looked at the covers. The first one seemed cool and I figured I might give it a shot and I had already read *The Catcher in the Rye* two years ago and I figured I could read it again, but the last one was pushing it.

I mean, come on. Right on the cover it said *Winner of the Nobel Prize in Literature*. I held it up when my mom walked by my room and said, "This is a bit of a reach, Mom. Baby steps, please." And she pretty much laughed. Then she said, "Baby steps are good, Joel."

TEXT FROM JOEL TO PRINCIPAL REDMAN 1:32 a.m.

Do they have a Nobel Prize for list making? 'Cause if they do Eli should get it. You know Eli Wells? The girl who tries to fix everyone and everything?

TEXT FROM JOEL TO PRINCIPAL REDMAN 1:43 a.m.

If we got Harleys either the Night Rod Specials or Low Riders it would save $679,000 and in case you're thinking that the girls won't like motorcycles I checked with Harley Davidson and they did a study and girls who ride motorcycles feel twice as happy and four times sexier after they get the bikes. So pretty much that sews it up. We should get Harleys.

TEXT FROM JOEL TO ANDY 1:56 a.m.

Pretty much we're all getting Harleys.
Either Night Rod Specials or Low Riders.

TEXT FROM JOEL TO ANDY 1:58 a.m.

Girls on Harleys feel four times more sexy than when they were girls not on Harleys. I mean, come on, we have to get Harleys.

TEXT FROM JOEL TO ANDY 2:07 a.m.

I'm reading *The Outsiders* by S. E. Hinton.
You would like it. I mean, really.

23

ONCE, SPINDINI TOLD ME AND ELI

that when you were in the armed forces and killed people for a living so you could keep other people alive and pave the road for democracy and freedom it was hard to take a real job when you were discharged.

He said that when you see little kids get shot or suicide bombers blow up crowds of people in a marketplace or have to hide for eight hours straight crouched against the wheel well of a Humvee with night goggles on and your gun pointed in one direction with orders to *shoot if you see anything fucking move*, it's hard to decide if you want to be a plumber or a florist or maybe go back to school to learn to be a podiatrist when you come back home.

That pretty much explained why Spindini was a permanent fixture at the soup kitchen. He had said it was one of those "goddamned vicious cycles."

At this point we were sitting with the Colonel and he told us that someone told him that the new guy with the two missing fingers who didn't talk got a Purple Heart and was a real hero in Iraq even though you couldn't tell that now, what with him not talking and that shopping cart full of shit, and me and Eli looked at each other because we were both shocked to hear that Rooster was a hero. I looked around and Rooster wasn't here yet but I noticed Spindini was sitting by himself eating a piece of cake by the door and then the Colonel spotted him too and leaned in close and told us that Spindini was extra messed up because he shot one of his buddies in Afghanistan by mistake. The Colonel said that the army didn't know about it, just Spindini and him and the dead guy and everyone else in his platoon and Spindini's wife, who left him, and his priest and maybe God and now me and Eli.

The Colonel called it "friendly fire."

I said, "It doesn't sound friendly to me," and I wasn't trying to be disrespectful. The Colonel said it just meant you shot someone you were friendly with or not even friendly with but who was just on the same side as you were on in the war and probably didn't even know. And after the Colonel explained it, Eli just stood up and got Spindini a second piece of cake even though she wasn't supposed to. She said she did it because it was the kind with chocolate frosting and sprinkles and he liked that the best.

Then, later, when Benj was clearing plates and I was emptying the trash, he came over to me and said, "Hey, Joel, are you going to Alison Newbury's party on Friday?" And I said, "No," mainly because I was thinking about the war in Iraq and suicide bombers and Rooster's Purple Heart and Spindini killing his buddy with friendly fire.

It's hard to go to parties when you think about things like what it would be like to shoot your buddy by mistake or sit wedged up against a wheel well of a Humvee with orders to shoot anything that fucking moves. Besides, it wasn't really a real party anyway because it was going to be held in the woods behind Alison's house, not *in her house*, and it was BYOE plus ten—which means *Bring Your Own Everything* including alcohol and drugs and snacks and whatnot, plus ten dollars presumably to pay for Alison's alcohol and drugs and snacks and whatnot since she was having the party but supplying the woods only.

It was a good thing that I didn't go to Alison's woods party 'cause the cops were there waiting for everyone on account of the fact that Alison went retro and printed up a flyer and ran off five hundred copies at Staples and handed them out to everyone at school and kids read them and then dropped them on the floor and put them in trash cans everywhere. They were all over, in the hallways by the lockers and in the trash in the classrooms—there were so many on the floors and seats of the school buses that the bus company called the school to complain—and someone handed one to one of the aides in the cafeteria by mistake and one person left one right on Mrs. Plummer's desk which was the worst place to leave it since she was the secretary to the principal. The cops staked out the woods and were waiting for everyone to arrive at 9:00 p.m. and then they confiscated all the drugs and alcohol and called everyone's parents and Alison was basically screwed.

Half the school was now grounded for the rest of their lives.

Except for Eli, who would never go to a party like that and was probably at home making food for shut-ins or one of those other things she did that made her such a good person, and then there was me who stayed home to read Jace *Winnie-the-Pooh* and think about what it would be like to be told to sit in the dark and shoot anything that fucking moves and then to come home and try to choose a new career like house painter or schoolteacher or maybe gun salesman or arms dealer or golf pro. I read the chapter where Pooh and Piglet are trying to catch a Heffalump in a very Cunning Trap and the whole time I was thinking about whether Pooh should be wearing underpants and what color they should be and then when Jace fell asleep I went to the garage and took the gun out of the plastic bag and unwrapped it from the rag and sat in the back by the bricks on the cement floor in the dark pointing that gun in one direction telling myself not to breathe too loud and to shoot *anything that fucking moves* and it was pitch-black and my hand was twitching and the hammer wasn't cocked but there was one bullet in the chamber and I knew that 'cause I put it there. I had to check how to load a gun on the internet 'cause Jackson didn't have any guns, even though you would think he would, but Jesus, Mary said, "Not with kids in the house, Jackson."

I got jumpy after only fifteen minutes, not eight hours, and I was scared even though I was in my own garage in my own yard at my own house and there were no enemy soldiers and nobody was trying to kill me and there were no dead kids or suicide bombers or marketplaces blowing up and none of my buddies were sitting near me with guns pointed in all directions, there was just me wondering about friendly fire and what it would look like in my yard if I had night-vision goggles on.

I was just there with my own thoughts and that was way scarier than I thought it would be.

After two hours I put the gun down and texted Eli, *A lot more soldiers than you'd think died in friendly fire accidents in Operation Iraqi Freedom not just the guy Spindini shot by mistake and you get put to death by hanging in public in Iran for reading a book with a gay person in it and I just read Winnie-the-Pooh to Jace.* Then I typed, *And we should tell Mrs. T that homeless people can get SNAP benefits and that's basically a card with free money from the government for food if you don't make enough money to buy food and don't have food and I have a gun with a bullet in it and we should be really grateful to Spindini and the Colonel and Rooster and all of them because they are fighting for our right to free speech and I am going to read all of the banned books I can.* And then I saved the whole thing to draft and just typed, *Do you get an Auto F for saying what you really feel?* and sent it.

Eli texted back, *Joel, just raise your hand first and STOP WORRYING ABOUT AUTO Fs*, and I typed, *I'm trying*, and she sent back five emojis of yellow hearts that were bigger than any I had ever seen in my entire life.

I didn't know what that meant and my hand froze and I searched for the right thing to text back but my choices were between real words—and I didn't know any good ones—or stupid pictures of a thumbs-up or a cute dog or a flower or an airplane or a traffic light or gas pump or french fries or a wink face. So I sent her an emoji of a piece of cake with exploding sprinkles but I had to put the gun down again to do that. Then I typed, *Thanks*, and she wrote, *For what*? And I wrote, *For making me feel better*, but I didn't tell her I had been holding a gun and was worried about things like SNAP benefits for free food and talking animals and underpants and Humvees and friendly fire and what happens when your buddy dies. Then I put the gun back in the bag in its hiding place and went back into the house and found Jace asleep in my bed and when I tried to carry him back to his room he woke up and said, "I can't sleep in my bed 'cause it's wet," so I put him back in my bed and then climbed into the top bunk and tried not to think about anything at all.

TEXT FROM JOEL TO ELI 2:35 a.m.

I like that you make so many lists.

Maybe we could get together and I could make lists with you.

I mean, if that would make you feel better.

TEXT FROM JOEL TO ELI 2:42 a.m.

I have bad thoughts all the time. So I pretty much smash things. And I have a gun in my garage and sometimes when I'm done smashing things I just hold the gun and have bad thoughts.

The gun doesn't help. I still have the bad thoughts. So it's probably a good thing that you write things down. I mean, it's probably better than smashing things or getting a gun.

TEXT FROM JOEL TO ANDY 2:47 a.m.

Now I have two new sicknesses. One's called collywobbles and the other is exploding head syndrome. The first one is basically a stomachache and the second one is a bad headache. I'm pretty sure. I mean, I have all the symptoms. For both. My mom just said take Tylenol, you're fine, Joel, but she doesn't know what she's talking about.

TEXT FROM JOEL TO ANDY 2:53 a.m.

I read books now.

A lot of them.

Like all the time.

It's weird.

Just so you know.

24

EVERY WEDNESDAY

when Rooster came into the soup kitchen, if Eli saw him first, she would find me and whisper, "Joel, I see the bear," and that would be my cue to go watch his stuff.

Then, every time right after he finished eating, I would walk back inside and go over to him and ask, "Can I get you anything else?" even though I knew he didn't speak, but just because you never know.

He never answered and he always looked away like I made him nervous and uncomfortable and once, when Benj was watching me try to talk to him, afterward, Benj said, "Hey, man, maybe you should just leave him alone," and I said, "Shut up, Benj." Then he said, "The guy just wants to eat and get out of here. It would be better if you didn't say anything to him at all," and I said, "Shut the fuck up, Benj, I mean it." And then I said, "Can I have your socks?" and Benj said, "Okay."

The next Wednesday after Eli found me and whispered, "Joel, I see the bear," and I went outside to stand next to his cart, when Rooster was finished eating I walked over just like I usually did and leaned on the table and said, "Can I get you anything else?" But this time when he wouldn't look at me I decided to try something different and I leaned in even closer and whispered, "Hold up one finger if you can hear me."

Rooster didn't look up but his right hand was on the table in a fist and I watched as he slowly lifted his hand and unfolded his pointer finger and held it up for me just a few inches above the table. Then he quickly put his hand back down and made a fist again.

My heart sped up and I slid onto the bench across from him and tried to make eye contact but he still wouldn't look at me. Then I whispered real low, "Okay, one finger is yes and two fingers is no."

Nothing.

"Is it okay that I'm talking to you now?"

One finger. Then a fist.

I was thinking, *Holy f-ing shit!* and kept the questions coming.

"Is it okay that I bring stuff to where you are living?"

One finger. Then a fist.

"Do you need anything?"

One finger. No fist.

I sat there across from him with my heart racing like the engine in a car trying to climb a hill in the wrong gear. "Can you tell me what you need?"

Two fingers. *No*.

I sat back. Exhaled real slow. "But you need something?"

He folded one finger back under and there it was. His pointer finger screaming right at me, *Yes, I need something*.

Since the question of what he needed couldn't be answered with yes or no, I said, "Don't leave," then ran to my backpack and pulled out a pen and a piece of paper and then ran back and sat down across from him again and tried to hand it to him but he just pushed the pen and paper back at me.

At this point he was real agitated and pissed off. His face twitching and his eyes darting around the room like he was looking for a way out.

I looked over and saw Benj watching me from the kitchen door, then Rooster stood up, stepped back, and banged into a chair as he made his way to the exit, pulled the door open, stepped outside, took his cart, and headed up the block. I followed after him, but he gestured with his hand for me to go away.

I followed him for a bit more but stopped where the sidewalk ends.

Then I hung back and just watched as he pushed his shopping cart down the length of road that would eventually take him home.

JACEY HAD A MONSTER

in his closet.

And when I got home that night after working in the soup kitchen, Jackson and Jesus, Mary were arguing about how to handle it because it had gotten out of control. First, Jace had to have his bedroom door open a little, and then the door had to be open all the way with his light on and the hall light on, and then Pop had to do a "monster check" by opening his closet and looking under the bed and even with all that Jace ended up in my bed or sleeping on the floor in my room curled up in the corner with Lacey. Lacey wasn't supposed to be sleeping in my room either and while Jesus, Mary and Jackson had given up on that one, they both put all four of their paws down about Jace sleeping with the dog. Jackson said, "Jesus, Mary, he's got a perfectly good bed in a perfectly good room without any monsters. Why would he sleep with the dog?"

She said, "You sure, Jackson?"

"Am I sure about what?"

"That there are no monsters?"

"Jesus, Mary!"

Then my mom said, "I'm just saying that if Jace thinks there are monsters that makes them real to him."

I asked Jace, "Why can't you just stay in your bed?" when he came into my room later that night and climbed into my bottom bunk when I was still up doing homework. I was sitting in the New York Yankees beanbag chair that Jackson got me one Christmas 'cause he really wanted it for himself and then I added, "There's no such thing as monsters."

"Yes, there is too."

"Is too what?"

"Monsters."

"Show me," I said.

"You can't see them."

"If they're real we could see them."

Then Jace ran back to his room and brought in a whole bunch of books like *Where the Wild Things Are* and *The Minpins* and I said, "But these monsters are make-believe. They're just books."

"No. They're true. And there are too monsters."

"So now there are two monsters?" I asked holding up two fingers.

"Youuuuuu . . ." he said, and then he started to hold his breath, which was one of those things we were supposed to ignore just like the bed wetting and the F bomb so it would extinguish but when he would do it Pop would say, "Jesus, Mary, he's turning blue, shouldn't we do something?" And before she could even answer I would just hop up and tickle Jace and end the whole thing because you can't not breathe if someone is tickling you.

Then Jacey did that pointer finger thing that means come with me, took me by the hand, and brought me to his room and put his finger over his lips and said, "Shhhhh!" Then he opened his closet door and moved some stuff out of the way and in the far back corner of his closet he pointed to a pair of blue sneakers that I hadn't seen since last summer and probably didn't fit him anymore. I leaned forward and saw that inside both sneakers was . . .

What the . . . ?

"Dog kibble," Jacey said. "I'm sure."

Then, when I didn't say a thing, Jace said, "I didn't put it there and Lacey didn't put it there because she doesn't have hands."

He had a point.

"And in the night I hear the monster eating."

I said, "Jesus, Jacey, it's not a monster. It's a mouse."

He said, "No way."

I said, "Way." Then I said, "Come with me and I'll prove it."

I took him into my room, where we researched mousetraps online and then we went downstairs to the kitchen and I asked Pop to drive us to town the next day after school. He said, "What for?" And I said, "For a secret mission," and he said, "No." Then I said, "It might solve the monster problem," and he said, "Really?" I said, "It will just take a ride to town and thirteen dollars and ninety-five cents."

"And Jace will sleep in his bed?"

Jace said, "No way!"

I said, "Way! But it might take a couple of days to work."

Then Jackson leaned back in his chair and said, "And you won't tell me what you're doing?"

"Nope. Secret brother project."

Jacey lit up. You could see the happiness spread over his face like it was paint spilled from a can.

I was learning that some problems were easier to fix than others.

26

THE NEXT DAY AFTER SCHOOL

I ignored the gun-and-badge-hidden-in-the-garage problem and the 41.2-million-hungry-people-in-the-US problem and the Rooster-won't-talk problem and the banned-book problem and the Joel-is-too-short problem and set my sights on something I *could* fix like the monster-in-Jacey's-closet problem.

After he got home from the station Pop drove me and Jace to Brinkley's on Main, which was one of those hardware stores that's been in the same family for generations. When we pulled up in the front Jackson asked me how we were going to solve the monster problem by buying something in a hardware store and I said, "That's easy. We're getting a monster trap," and Jace hopped out after me and added, "A very cunning trap!"

Brinkley's on Main is a real authentic-looking, old New England country store with a big front porch, a bell on the door, rakes and brooms in the front window, old-fashioned penny candy in big glass jars, and an old dog that didn't so much guard the place as own it. Yellow lab named Beau with a bit of gray beard sprouting around the muzzle and arthritis in his hind legs so bad that going up and down the stairs out front was something Beau reserved for opening and closing only. He still looked up every time the bell on the door rang and gave a small thump of his tail when he saw you enter, but just enough to indicate you were welcome to come inside. Old Beau no longer had the enthusiasm to hop on up and give you a proper hello and a face lick like I remembered him doing when I was little.

I took Jace downstairs at Brinkley's and we found the tiniest no-kill animal trap they sold. Olson model number RT-3040-2. Got a package of two for $13.95. It was labeled for catching chipmunks, as nobody but me wanted to catch a mouse alive. Then as long as we were there, and since Jackson gave me a twenty-dollar bill, I went over to the nail and screw bins and started looking for something to hold pieces of plywood together that might work better than rusty wire and rope, thinking that maybe I could help Rooster fix up his place, when a man I didn't know came over to me and said, "You're Jackson's boy."

"Yes, sir," I said, not recognizing him even a tiny bit.

"Your dad's been working on my truck for more years than I can count."

"Yes, sir."

"Been spending some time up in the woods behind the Richardsons' farm have you?"

It was more of an observation or statement of fact than a question.

I picked up a ¾-inch self-driving flat-head screw and examined it like it was the eleventh wonder of the world and Jacey ran back up the stairs to play with Beau.

"I've been workin' up at the Richardsons' for goin' on ten years now," he continued. "Handyman, part-time farmer. Drive the Mr. and

Mrs. to the doctor now and again. Slap some paint around. Things like that."

I grabbed a small paper bag and started filling it with ¾-inch self-driving flat-head screws and he said, "If some eggs go missin' from one of the hen houses no one's likely to notice."

I looked up.

He nodded.

"You mean . . ."

"I mean that if a few dozen eggs go missing each week no one's likely to notice. Not the Richardsons, and not me."

I was thinking, *What the fuck are you saying?* but basically I ReThought and said, "Yes, sir, I understand," even though I was not the least bit sure that I did.

"And there's a field of asparagus behind the green barn that doesn't even get harvested anymore. Just left there to go to seed. Close to half an acre that goes unpicked every season, in fact. They're perennials. That means that they come up every year on their own. Grow like the dickens, too. Can't pick 'em fast enough. They wouldn't go noticed if they disappeared either. Coming up now, as a matter of fact."

"Asparagus?"

"You do know what asparagus are, don't you, son?"

And I said, "Of course I know what fucking asparagus are. I haven't been living in a fucking underground bunker." I just left off the "Of course" and the two "fucking"s and the part about "living underground in a bunker," so I basically said, "Yes, sir."

Then I added, "But you're saying that if I were—"

"I'm not saying anything, but people gotta eat. One way or another."

"Yes, sir."

"If you're looking for something to hold some boards together you might want to look into brackets. Like these here," he said, holding up something that looked damned perfect for what I had in mind. "I gotta run now. You have a nice day. Say hi to your dad for me. Name's Miller."

Mr. Miller started to walk away and then he turned back around. "I ran into Brice Torrington the other day," he said. "She said that you volunteer at the soup kitchen up on Hendricks."

"On Wednesdays."

"Right, Wednesdays . . . Ever had a poached egg on a bed of steamed asparagus?"

"No, sir, I have not."

"Just about the best damned thing in the world. You might want to try it sometime. And I'm betting that the patrons up at Brice's soup kitchen might enjoy it, too."

I didn't say anything, but I nodded my head.

We looked at each other long and hard after that and then he turned and went up the stairs. I could see him as he bent down and gave Jacey and old Beau a pat on their heads. Mr. Miller got the short tail thump and then I watched as he gave old Beau a tummy rub and Beau then went the extra mile and gave Mr. Miller a little wet nose nuzzle on the palm of his hand as payment in kind. Which reminded me that there's just something about dogs. They always seem to know who the good guys are.

27

ME AND JACEY CAUGHT OURSELVES

one fine monster.

Right there in the monster trap that we set up in his closet after we got home from Brinkley's. I had promised to sleep in his bed with him or at least stand guard that night until we heard it go snap, which was not the broken-neck snap of a regular mousetrap but the closing of the gate on a tiny cage kind of snap, but it went snap almost immediately after we set it up and then Jace peed all over himself and he said, "See, there are too monsters," and I said, "Let's go see what we caught." Jace looked ridiculous 'cause he was wearing those feet-y pajamas with his toes sticking out and now they were all wet because him peeing all the time was another one of those problems Jesus, Mary thought would extinguish if we ignored it, so I didn't even mention the fact that he needed to change. I think he really expected to find a character from one of his books like a real Minpin or maybe even a Hobbit or one of the Borrowers right there in the little trap. And when we opened the closet door and cleared a path to the back, there he was.

Our monster.

"Not so scary after all," I said to Jace.

The whole plan backfired though 'cause I was planning on letting the mouse monster go somewhere far off in the woods so he wouldn't find his way back, but now that Jace saw how cute he was he wanted to keep him.

Which is how we got Scabbers.

"That's what Ron called his mouse in Harry Potter," Jace told me.

I had to take his word on that on account of the fact that I hadn't read any of the Harry Potter books.

Yep. I'm that guy. The only person in the fucking world who hasn't read even one Harry Potter book.

On the plus side, Jacey slept in his own bed after that with the door mostly closed and the lights mostly off with only a night light on. But the problem was that the clock was ticking on how long this setup was going to last.

Now I had two things to hide.

The mouse from the Harry Potter books in Jace's closet and a gun in the garage.

TEXT FROM JOEL TO ANDY 8:22 p.m.

Jacey and I have a pet mouse. You would think it's dumb but it's cool.

TEXT FROM JOEL TO ANDY 1:50 a.m.

Okay. I have some suspicious new symptoms.

Pretty much it's onychomycosis.

Which is toenail fungus. It's just not on my toenails. So it's weird.

But doctors in the Netherlands are working on a cure so don't worry. I emailed one of them and attached a picture. It's gross.

WHENEVER WE WERE WAITING FOR MR. STANLEY,

Benj was always asking anyone who was standing around what-if driving questions.

This time it was, "What if you're driving down a steep hill toward an intersection with heavy traffic and you lose your brakes and there's a tractor trailer sitting directly in front of you and the traffic isn't moving because of a red light and you're going to hit the truck broadside if you don't do something fast to avoid it. Do you:

A. Lean on the horn and hope that the traffic will move enough to let you in and then make a wide, arced ninety-degree turn to absorb some of your speed and then make a second arced turn, this one on the banked entrance ramp into the Burger King parking lot and then crash the car into the snowbank that the plows piled up in the back to absorb any remaining speed, or

B. As you are careening down the hill, but before you hit the truck broadside, slam the car into reverse to jam the transmission then pull on the parking brake and then turn the wheel a sharp one hundred and eighty degrees so you crash into the trees because the timing on option A is impossible?"

Alex B. Renner said, "Holy shit that's a lot of detail. Who says there's a Burger King with a snowbank or—"

"Jesus," I said, interrupting him. "Who says there's *anything*? He just made the whole thing up, so go with it."

"Then if Kutchner can make stuff up so can I. And I would either launch the parachute out the back of the Batmobile I was driving to bring it to a stop or accelerate then engage the Batmobile wings that I had Alfred install and then I'd fly my brakeless car right over the tractor trailer and land at Teterboro Airport, which is where I park the Batplane."

I said, "Dude, you can't even drive a Ford Fiesta, so I don't think you could handle the Batmobile or the Batplane."

Then Benj said, "That's it. Alex B. Renner can't play."

"Okay, Benj," I said. "How's this? I'd pull the emergency brake, slip the car into neutral, then turn off the ignition to slow it down, 'cause putting it into reverse won't actually do anything, and then I'd exit the vehicle before impact."

"You mean jump out?"

"More of a roll. Put my head down and shoulder into it."

"That's cool, Joel. I didn't think of that. That you could jump out maybe before the crash. Thanks."

"No problem, man. Can I have your socks?"

"What?"

"Your socks. Can I have them?"

"Okay."

Benj sat down to take his socks off.

Then Alex B. Renner said, "What the hell is going on between you two?"

But neither one of us answered.

I was getting two pairs of socks a week from Benj at this point, which was good on account of the fact that I had no socks of my own left and Jesus, Mary was now saying to Jackson, "This is ridiculous, Jackson! What has happened to all of *your* socks?" And he would say, "Jesus, Mary, how the hell should I know? *You* do the laundry."

29

I INVITED ELI TO GO COLLECT EGGS

and pick asparagus with me at the Richardsons' farm.

With her hand on her hip and suspicion on her face she said, "Why do I have to wear camouflage, Joel?"

And I said it was on account of the fact that it was a crime to let food rot on the ground when people were hungry. We were standing by our lockers and school had just let out and she looked at the camouflage shirt and pants I was holding out for her to take that Jackson bought one year for my mom on their anniversary but my mom refused to wear because she said hunting fatigues were the worst anniversary gift in the history of the world, and Eli said, "Joel, are you saying that we are going to be *stealing*?" And I said, "No way, I got permission." But I left off the part about it not being from the actual owner of the farm and she said, "So, we are *not* stealing, right?" And I said, "Pretty much that would be a no." And she said, "What on earth does that mean? Because to me it sounds like you're not sure and you not being sure sounds a whole lot like stealing." And I said, "Trust me. The two of us collecting eggs and picking asparagus from some run-down farm to bring to the soup kitchen is something that God would approve of. I am certain of that."

I think I pretty much got her with the God argument because she took the clothes from me and went into the girls' bathroom and put them on and then we took the bus that dropped off at the edge of town and the kids all stared at us because it was weird that we were dressed in camouflage like army rangers or hunters and then we got off the bus and walked up to the Richardsons' farm and we entered on the same path Rooster used to push his cart on and I made a wide berth around his shack so Eli wouldn't see it because that would have broken her heart. Then we snuck into the henhouse, which was not hard to find because of all the clucking and crowing, and gathered dozens of eggs that we put in the crates that I found stacked on the side of the building. After a few minutes I looked up at Eli and said, "Have you ever had a poached egg on a bed of steamed asparagus?" and she burst out laughing 'cause that sounded like a ridiculous thing for me to have said and then she looked right at me and smiled and said, "No, I have not."

There were little baby chicks running around at our feet and the sun was streaming in through the rafters and it made her look so pretty and I said, "Well, you're in for a real treat, then, 'cause it's just about the best thing on earth," and she said, "Joel, it can't be better than cake," and I wanted to kiss her. Like *really* wanted to kiss her.

But I didn't dare because if she got mad—or threw up—it would ruin everything. Plus, we were in a henhouse and there were chickens squawking and it stunk worse than Kutchner's gym locker and I didn't want our first kiss to be in a place like that. So I said, "We are going to serve poached eggs on asparagus at the soup kitchen tomorrow." And Eli said, "Joel Higgins, you are too cute." And I was going to tell her again that *Too Cute* was a TV show about kittens and puppies that

Jacey watched with my mom but instead I stepped in closer and was about to tell her that I was in love with her but I ReThought and saved those words as a draft just like that kiss and all of those text messages and I said, "Let's go pick asparagus before we get caught in here." And Eli said, "Joel, I thought we weren't stealing?" And I said, "Technically, we're not." And Eli said, "Joel!" and then she ran out of the henhouse without the crates full of the eggs she had collected and I had to carry out hers and mine and then run after her. I carefully stacked the crates on the side of one of the outbuildings, and then after I caught up with her, it took us a while to find the asparagus field because we didn't really know what we were looking for even though Mr. Miller said it was behind the green barn. That's because when we finally found it, it didn't look like much at all. There were just asparagus sticking up out of the ground and they were half-hidden in the tangle of grass and weeds. I mean, I was expecting something that looked like a garden with neat rows and obvious plants but that's not what we found. The asparagus we see in the store is literally the entire plant and it grows directly out of the ground with no extra leaves or anything. It was the funniest vegetable thing I had ever seen in my entire life. I mean, try to imagine a field of carrots where the carrots didn't grow underground; they were just naked carrots sticking up out of the dirt with no green stuff at all. How ridiculous would that be?

We picked as much as we could carry.

Heaps of them.

We just snapped them off and filled up the six plastic bags that I had brought from home.

I kept looking up at Eli the whole time we were at the farm and she looked so happy. Like maybe she could like me.

Or be a farmer.

That was probably more like it.

I decided that she was definitely happy because of the farmer thing.

Not the Joel thing.

There was no Joel thing.

I had to keep reminding myself of that when I got confused.

Or overly optimistic.

Or both.

TEXT FROM JOEL TO PRINCIPAL REDMAN 5:16 p.m.

If we go ahead with the whole plow-up-the-teachers'-parking-lot thing, I think we should plant asparagus. And maybe we could raise chickens in the gym.

TEXT FROM JOEL TO PRINCIPAL REDMAN 5:44 p.m.

Maybe we should bulldoze the football field and grow food for the hungry there too.
Then kids could learn farming instead of football.
I mean, come on. Football basically sucks.

TEXT FROM JOEL TO PRINCIPAL REDMAN 9:44 p.m.

We should really do the football-field-conversion-to-a-farm thing. Maybe make the soccer field into a farm too. And we might as well do the track, as long as we're at it. I was thinking we could grow potatoes and strawberries maybe. Or wheat and corn.

And we should do the whole car/bus-swap-up thing too.

TEXT FROM JOEL TO ANDY 10:11 p.m.

I have a few new symptoms. They're pretty nasty. I won't get into them here. But just so you know.

30

MRS. T WAS IMPRESSED

with the food we might possibly have stolen a bit from the Richardsons' farm, being that we had permission from Mr. Miller, but not Mr. or Mrs. Richardson.

She had Macy and Margaret poach all of the 132 eggs since seven broke and they steamed all of the eighteen pounds of asparagus for exactly four minutes. I insisted that they rinse them in cold water after cooking just like Martha Stewart suggested on her website and that we serve the eggs directly on top of the asparagus like Mr. Miller said to do and everyone said it was the best thing they had ever eaten in their entire lives and it was.

When Spindini was eating his asparagus and eggs he asked me and Eli to sit down with him, which was something he did a lot, but this time it seemed different. He was sitting alone and picking up the asparagus spears with his fingers and dipping them in the runny egg yolks and eating them slowly and I could see that he was enjoying every bite, but something seemed off with him. In between mouthfuls he said, "Sometimes during the day I sit home and just watch war movies on

TV, one after another." Then he shook his head from side to side and added, "The directors get it fucking wrong, every time, man. The actors' uniforms are too clean. That really fucking bothers me."

He looked straight ahead like he was somewhere else and Eli and I exchanged a glance. Then Spindini said, "Being a soldier is like going on an odyssey to a foreign place in a way that makes coming back home really hard. When you're sent back to the place that is supposed to be your home sometimes it doesn't feel like home anymore even though you speak the language and you lived there your entire fucking life. Even when your family is there and your girlfriend is waiting for you.

"When you come back home after being deployed, when your tour is up and you get shipped back to the states, it can seem different, so fucking different."

Eli and me were real quiet. I was pretty much looking at the floor and Eli couldn't decide where to look so her eyes kept jumping around the room like she was looking for a safe place to look but knew she wasn't going to find one.

"And the thing of it is, it's not so much because home changed, it's because *you* changed."

Eli started to say, "Can I get you anything else to eat, like . . ." But Spindini didn't hear her, so her voice just trailed off.

"That fucking place you were? Even though it was more awful than you could have ever imagined and there was a fucking war going on and the cities and towns were nothing but dust and rubble, it can feel more like home to you than home does."

He shook his head and then said, "When I got home? My girlfriend wanted me to look at wedding dresses." He stared off into the distance. "Jesus. Fucking wedding dresses!

"She held up a picture on her phone and asked me, 'Which one do you like better? The one with the pearled bodice or the one with the long train?' I'll never forget that.

"Then she told me that her friend Barbara got a new car. Then she complained that her boss ate the same sandwich every day. She thought *that* was really annoying. Man, I just looked at her with a blank stare because it was all something that I couldn't understand and I fucking wanted to tell her that there are places, the places I went to, that are so hot and covered in so much sand that you can't see clearly or breathe."

I looked up from the floor and Eli caught my eye and we exchanged a look that said we didn't know what to do and we were scared where this was headed but Spindini kept going like this was a train wreck that had to happen and we were gonna watch it whether we liked it or not.

"And you want to tell your girlfriend that when you were there you couldn't shower for weeks and they warn you that if you're stationed at a post and you sit too long in the same position tucked inside a tank that's protecting a supply convoy or crouched behind a road embankment armed with a RPG rocket launcher with fire coming at you from all sides you can get deep vein thrombosis and a clot can travel to your brain or your lungs and kill you. Just for doing your job and fucking sitting there. And you learn on day one that the soldier's creed is *no man left behind* and that you chamber your last round so you can't be taken alive and the first thing you do if your hand is blown off is apply a tourniquet so you don't bleed out. And I wanted to tell her that you're never safe, even when you're sleeping and that sometimes supplies are so low that you have to make your own armor—hillbilly armor we called it—which means that you weld sheets of old rusty steel to the inside doors of the vehicle you'll be riding in so just maybe you won't die. And I want to tell her that things can just blow up with no notice even if you're just walking in a village trying to help people or are part of a caravan delivering supplies just driving up a dusty road littered with checkpoints and the skeletons of abandoned, burned-out military vehicles. I wanted to tell her that everyone looks like a civilian even if they are the enemy and carrying guns or planting IEDs and trying to kill you."

Then Spindini paused and picked up the last asparagus on his plate and I looked up and Eli was wiping away tears and Spindini said, "This is delicious by the way." And then he got that far-off look again and said, "IEDs are improvised explosive devices, which are bombs hidden in cars and rucksacks or on the side of the road or in a kid's backpack." And his hands were shaking and his face was sweating when he said, "And there are little kids, little five-year-olds, running around and they start looking like the enemy and you can't tell who to save and who to kill because they all look the same because they're just *people*, just like you and me, but you can't tell who is an enemy anymore and, man alive, you want to tell your girlfriend this in a language that she can understand because you fucking know she can't understand, so you say to her, imagine you are at Target and you're pushing your cart and trying to decide if you need to buy a garden hose or new sheets or wondering if you are out of paper towels and then there is an explosion so loud you can't hear anything but you feel it reverb in your chest and you can't see a thing through all that dust and then there is a second blast. . . ."

Eli put her hand on Spindini's back and I stood up knowing that I should get help but wondering from who and he kept going. "This time the blast is in the sheet department and then there's another in the toy department and then the whole store is just gone and your buddies are gone and you are gone or maybe just some of you is gone or maybe it looks like you are all there but then the doctors say they don't have the parts they need to make you whole again."

I stood there shaking and sweating and said, "Do you want me to get the colonel or Mrs. T or . . ."

Spindini looked straight up at me and he said, "A quarter of the homeless in America are veterans of wars fought in foreign lands that destroyed their homes and families even though not a single shot was fired here. It's like the nuclear fallout and radiation of war that we won't talk about."

I wiped the back of my hand across my eyes and said, "Is that why you went back to Iraq so many times? Because home didn't feel like home anymore?" but Spindini didn't answer.

He looked down at his plate and said, "Thank you for the food."

I backed up, knocking over two chairs by accident in the process, and said, "Thank you for your service." Then I walked away because I knew what I just said wasn't nearly enough.

But the thing of it was, even though those words I just said were nothing but a shopping cart full of shit, they were all that I had, and I had to hope that made them worth something after all.

Benj intercepted me on my way to the kitchen and said, "Joel, are you going to Chris Williams's party?" and I said, "No," and he said, "But—" and I said, "No," and stepped back to get away from him and knocked a plate of food onto the floor by mistake. When I went to clean up the mess Eli was at my side helping.

When we were done she followed me into the back and she was crying.

TEXT FROM JOEL TO PRINCIPAL REDMAN 4:30 a.m.

Have you ever had a poached egg on top of steamed asparagus? 'Cause if you did you'd plow up the parking lot, plant asparagus, and put chickens in the gym.

TEXT FROM JOEL TO PRINCIPAL REDMAN 4:34 a.m.

And if you came to the soup kitchen up on Hendricks Street and you sat down with some of the guys you'd figure out how to do something to help the veterans. And stop war. And grow more food.

31

THE NEXT DAY AT SCHOOL

Benj said if we were going to go to Burning Man we should get tickets soon.

I said, "Jesus, Benj, I told you I wasn't going."

Benj said that the tickets cost $390 each plus $80 to bring a car or truck in and when you get there you go to Walmart and buy all sorts of snacks and weird shit like costumes and Vaseline and licorice and face paint and then you ride a bike in the desert with goggles on because there is so much sand that it gets in your eyes and you can sleep in a tent or an RV or a yurt. He said seventy thousand people attend and it's like a giant campout with crazy people.

Eli had her phone out and she said seventy thousand is more than the population of Yuba City, California; Youngstown, Ohio; Waterloo, Iowa; Temple, Texas; Taylor, Michigan; and Utica, New York.

And I said, "What the hell is a yurt?"

And Benj said it's a really cool tent made for the desert and we'll have our driver's licenses by the summer, so we could probably go and that Black Rock City, Nevada, which is the name of the temporary city where Burning Man is held, is 2,691.1 miles from Rockland County if you measured it from his aunt's driveway on Adams Street. Then he said, "We'll miss the first two days of senior year but it will be worth it because it's like living on Mars with people from the future."

I said, "I'm not doing that, missing the first two days of senior year."

Then I said, "Where the hell are we going to get almost two thousand dollars and a truck and a yurt?"

Benj said, "The pennies and geometric progression."

I said, "Oh, that explains it."

Benj said he started with one penny six days ago and now he has sixty-four cents. In four days he'll have $10.24. Two days after that, $40.96. The day after that, $81.92. Day eighteen, $1,310.72. Then he said that on day nineteen he would have $2,621.44, which was more than enough for the tickets and the yurt and the Walmart stuff and gas. Then he said, "So in twelve days we will be fully funded. We will have eight hundred and sixty dollars for tickets and a thousand dollars for snacks and goggles and shit at Walmart." Then he said that the Burning Man website said to be prepared for fire, nakedness, and mutant vehicles. It said to bring fleece jackets, animal suits, and glow sticks. Also, animal ears, tails, wings, furry vests, sparkly clothes, and condoms.

Benj then said that the only problem was that you have to be eighteen or over to buy a ticket and attend the festival. But that maybe they won't check about the over-eighteen thing.

I said, "I think week two of your geometric progression is going to be a bit of an obstacle, too," but he didn't seem to hear me.

Then he said you didn't have to wear pants if you didn't want to because some people were naked in the pictures online and if you wanted to see naked girls wearing leather boots and hats made of ostrich feathers or if you liked fire and wanted to see a lot of stuff burn it was a good place to go. He said they burn a forty-foot-tall wood structure called "The Man," on the second-to-last night and people say it is the most powerful thing they've ever seen. Then Benj said there was a temple at Burning Man too, and it's not all about sex and nakedness and drugs, but he didn't want to talk about that part now.

I said, "Did you do the English homework?" And Benj said, "No. I'm going to fail English, so what would be the point?" And I said, "If you want to go to Burning Man you better not be in summer school." And he said, "Summer school will be over by then. I checked."

And then he said, "When you get home, google Burning Man and see how much fun we are going to have," and I said, "I told you, I'm not going."

32

OUR ENGLISH ASSIGNMENT

for Mr. Morgan that Benj didn't bother to do was to write a list of everything wrong with this country or with this class or with Mr. Morgan or with our parents or with ourselves.

It could be any overall category like teachers or the government or an institution that we perceived to be flawed. Mr. Morgan instructed us to put the things on the list that we *could fix* and also put things on the list that we thought that we *couldn't fix* and Eli had the best list out of everyone.

For starters it was seventy-two pages long and when Mr. Morgan looked it over he called it "fastidiously comprehensive" and she smiled. Eli had shown me the document before class and it included subcategories for the nuclear arms programs of North Korea and Iran as well as a long list of countries with human rights violations. She had separate headers for European, Russian, and Chinese colonialism; police brutality with subheads for the police forces of Ferguson, Missouri, and Baltimore, Maryland; and cities with policies to stop and frisk. Then there were categories for persecution based on gender identity, cloning, food insecurity, arms sales, gender parity, and global trade. She covered environmental concerns like overfishing the oceans, GMOs, and corn subsidies. Then there were prescription drug prices, the opiate epidemic, Chinese cyberhacking, high-fructose corn syrup, sexual harassment, carcinogens in toothpaste, and slavery. She covered everything from equal pay for women to child labor laws to fair treatment of immigrants to free speech and the closing of Guantanamo Bay. Then there was waterboarding, proper food labeling, and securing adequate funding for research on the Zika virus. That was just a sampling from the first thirteen pages. She had absolutely nothing in the column for "things she could not fix" and I suggested that she could put my name there, as I was a massive, unsolvable large-scale problem sort of like malaria or global warming.

Benj suggested that maybe I was just a giant, cosmic energy suck like a black hole.

I said, "Thanks, Benj," and gave him a look.

But Eli took our comments seriously and said she'd think about it.

For my list I only included minor annoyances, not because I didn't understand the assignment or have BIG grievances, because I did. But I just didn't want to share them with the class. I wanted to make a list of all the stuff Mr. Morgan taught us about free speech and banned books and all the stuff that Spindini had been telling us like the fact that almost one-quarter of the homeless in this country are veterans and that veterans can't get the medical care they need and sometimes they come home missing body parts and sometimes they come home with all of their body parts but still something big is missing or damaged or needs to be fixed and that we should make it feel like home for them when they get here so they won't want to go back to war because they feel more at home in a foreign war zone with their buddies than then they do here in America with their families. And I wanted to say that we don't make them feel like this is home mostly because we are all thinking about THE WRONG THINGS like if we have a cool car or who won the football game or if it's better to take the SATs in the spring or fall or whether the Yankees are better than the Mets, or if a pearled bodice is better than a long train on a wedding dress, instead of thinking about what it might be like to come home with parts of yourself missing. So my "things I want to solve" list for Mr. Morgan had stuff on it like there shouldn't be late fines at the library and there should be free chocolate-chip cookies in the cafeteria and maybe Mr. Morgan should lighten up on the Auto F policy because it's freaking everyone out and he never really uses it anyway and short guys should get to go out with tall girls if they want to. And then I made a list of all of the tall girl–short guy combos with subcategories:

First there was the movie star–movie star combo:

Daniel Radcliffe and Erin Darke

Seth Green and Clare Grant

Then there was the movie star–rocker combo:

Justin Bieber and Yovanna

And the iconic supermodel–short president of France combo:

Carla Bruni and Nicolas Sarkozy

And of course the supermodel girl–super-rich guy combo like:

Alessandra Ambrosio and

Jamie Mazur and, like, a gazillion others

And then I got depressed because there was a common thread, which was that tall girls only dated short guys if they were rich or famous or in a rock band or were hotshot bankers with mega yachts or the president of France. There wasn't a single short guy who worked at a gas station dating a tall perfect girl who made lists of everything wrong with the world and planned on fixing all of it. So I deleted the whole tall girl–short guy part and stuck with things like the fact that it was really annoying that they don't have chocolate milk in the cafeteria anymore.

Eli's list could have been sent to the president of the Red Cross or to the UN or Doctors Without Borders, or the Congress of the United States and mine could have been sent to absolutely no one unless there was a government agency in charge of filling up a Dumpster with pathetic, petty personal gripes. So I just ripped my list up and figured I deserved an Auto F but luckily for Benj and me Mr. Morgan didn't collect our homework this time. Mr. Morgan just said, "Read over the list you made because these lists may be the most important thing you will ever write, even though it may not seem that way right now. When you are sixteen years old you still feel the world is a place where you can fix everything, and everything seems possible to you, and that drive and ambition and blind optimism is the engine that drives important change."

When I looked over at Eli she was smiling like she had finally seen God for real and I thought, *It's a good thing that I ripped up my list*, because I don't want to read it years from now and look back and see that at my very best I was concerned about the broken yogurt machine in the cafeteria at Calf City High School in Rockland County and the absolutely abhorrent injustice of white milk.

Right before the class ended Benj leaned in close to me and whispered, "Now I understand why Eli makes lists all the time."

And I said, "Me too. I'd be making lists a lot, too, if I thought that I had to fix that much stuff."

Then Mr. Morgan said, "One more thing. A few parents complained about the subject matter of the books we've been reading this year, so there's a new policy that if we're going to read a book or have a discussion about anything that anyone might be uncomfortable with, I have to let you know ahead of time and give you a chance to opt out.

"This new policy is based on something called *the violence of words*. Meaning that some words and some stories can deal with content and language that can be so damaging that we have to protect you from experiencing it.

"So from now on I will warn you if there are any 'trigger words' or 'trigger topics' that could traumatize or offend any one of you because of a previous experience—or strongly held belief. I've been instructed to inform you that there will be a 'safe space' right next to Mrs. Plummer's office where you can go to shield yourself from that conversation if you feel that it will be too traumatic for you."

Then I raised my hand and got called on. I stood up and everyone looked at me because I never volunteered to talk and I said, "I thought the whole point was that we were supposed to be traumatized by violent words. That's how you learn."

Mr. Morgan said, "Me too. But some people believe students are fragile intellectual eggs and need to be offered a safe space to hide if a topic of conversation might be upsetting to them."

Benj blurted out, "You mean like if there are gay people in books?" And Mr. Morgan said, "Yes."

Then Paulie Pullman raised his hand and Mr. Morgan called on him and Paulie said, "So, if I don't want to read a book with a gay character in it I can go to Mrs. Plummer's office?"

"Yes, and you can color. I hear she has the large box of crayons."

Paulie got up and left the room and without raising my hand or getting permission I stood up again and called after him, "You're making a mistake." And then I turned to face Mr. Morgan and said, "Give me an Auto F."

And he said, "No."

And I said, "You have to. Speaking without being called on is on the Auto F list. . . ."

No one moved.

Not even Mr. Morgan.

And then he said, "Joel, sit down."

I kept standing there. I said, "But . . ."

He said, "Joel."

Then I finally slipped back into my seat.

There were still ten minutes left in class and everyone just stayed at their desks and thought about stuff, probably free speech and safe spaces and the violence of words. And some of us were thinking about other stuff like banned books and IEDs and Spindini and Eli.

Then the bell rang and Benj got up to leave and he walked over to me and said, "We're still going to Burning Man. Right?"

And I said, "Basically, that's still a no."

TEXT FROM JOEL TO PRINCIPAL REDMAN 1:24 a.m.

About that raise for Mr. Morgan. He should really get it.
Like now. Maybe use some of the bus/car-swap money.

If we got Zipcars instead of Corvettes and Camaros or Jeeps
or Harleys we could still ditch the buses and use the rest
of the money for Mr. Morgan's raise and for farming.

It should definitely be Zipcars. Or Harleys.
Either way. I'm good with both.

TEXT FROM JOEL TO ANDY 1:31 a.m.

My whole family is sick. My mom says we're fine and that I have
to stop worrying. I'm still pretty sure she has tuberculosis.
Jacey is a walking rash and Jackson's a mess. I'm thinking
sciatica, arthritis, high blood pressure, and colitis.
I pretty much have a brain tumor to go with the toenail fungus,
the collywobbles, and exploding head syndrome. I mean, a tumor
explains the headaches better than exploding head syndrome.
But I don't want you to worry. I'm just keeping you up to date.

WHILE WE WERE WAITING FOR MR. STANLEY

and the Driver's Ed car to pull around, which was going to take a while being that the seniors on the football team had carried it onto the tennis courts, there were some other kids nearby waiting for the track coach, and Benj was asking all of us one of his annoying what-if questions.

"Quick! You are in the right-hand lane of a four-lane highway with no median strip between the two sides to separate you from oncoming traffic and there's a police car with the lights on and its siren blaring barreling down on you from behind and a lady is walking on the shoulder of the highway with a dog, so you can't pull over and there's a tractor trailer in the left lane, so you can't switch lanes. Do you:

A. Hit the lady in order to pull over for the cop, or
B. Hit the tractor trailer to let the cop car through and save the lady?"

Alex B. Renner said, "Definitely B," and a really tall sophomore on the track team named Ralph something said, "What the fuck, man?

That means you would sideswipe the tractor trailer and end up dead." Then Alex B. Renner said, "Yeah, but I would never have to answer one of Kutchner's Driver's Ed what-ifs again."

Then some kid who I didn't even recognize who must have been a freshman who just moved here asked, "What does the lady walking on the side of the road look like?" and Benj said, "What difference does that make?" And the kid said, "If she was hot I wouldn't want to run her over, that's all."

Then Ron Henley chimed in and said, "Assume she looks like me."

Which was funny 'cause he was basically a fur factory and looked like a Neanderthal man had a baby with Bigfoot.

Then Charlie Watson, who was the fastest kid in the school, said, "Then I'd hit the lady."

Then Henley punched him on his shoulder. Not hard, but still.

Then another kid asked, "What kind of dog is it?" and someone else said, "Assume that it's a Rottweiler," and Alex B. Renner said, "If you just wait a few seconds until you pass the lady walking you could then pull to the side safely."

And Benj said, "Assume she's a fast walker."

"As in, she can walk fifty-five miles per hour?"

"Yes, she can walk *really* fast. Don't ruin the game."

Then Alex B. Renner said, "Well, then, if the car I was in *and* the tractor trailer *and* the lady *and* the Rottweiler were all moving at fifty-five miles per hour and I accelerated to sixty-five miles per hour I would be forty-four feet in front of the dog-walking lady *and* the tractor trailer in three seconds and I would have my choice of either crossing safely into the left lane in front of the truck *or* pulling into the breakdown lane in front of the lady who looks like Ron Henley and letting the police car by without colliding with the truck *or* hitting the hideous-looking lady who together with her dog can walk faster than anyone on earth."

Benj said, "Fuck, man, you ruined my story."

Then I said, "I would slam the car into reverse, plow ass-first into the cop car, do a one-hundred-and-eighty-degree turn and then speed in the opposite direction into oncoming traffic."

And Alex B. Renner said, "Who the hell would that help?"

And I said, "Nobody. I just wanted to make Benj happy."

But none of us, not Benj Kutchner, not the entire track team, not Joel Higgins, and not even Alex B. Renner were listening anymore on account of the fact that Olivia Beaumont and Cynthia Jackson just walked by in tight tank tops and itty-bitty track shorts and every last one of us forgot how to think.

Then I said, "Socks, Benj."

And he said, "Okay, Joel," and then he sat down to take his shoes off.

Then Alex B. Renner looked down at Benj on the sidewalk and said, "What the fuck?"

Then Eli showed up and she was looking at her phone and she blurted out, "In Alabama it's illegal to drive while blindfolded," then she burst out laughing. The track kids had all headed down to the field for practice and we were still standing outside on the sidewalk waiting for Mr. Stanley to pull up in the Driver's Ed car and he was now really late and Eli was still looking at her phone googling more weird driving laws and making one of her lists.

"No, it's not," I said. "You made that up."

"Did not."

I reached for her phone.

She stepped backward with her eyes glued to the screen.

"In Alaska it's illegal to tether a dog to the roof of a car and drive."

"Is not." I lunged left but she outstepped me.

"Of course it is, Joel. It can't be *legal* to tie a dog to the roof of a car."

"But it can't be an actual *law* that it's *illegal* either," I said as I almost got her hand. "Laws are not that specific or that stupid."

Reached and missed again.

"Yes, they are! In Arkansas it's against the law to honk a horn where cold drinks or sandwiches are served after nine p.m."

She was still staggering backward and I was still grabbing at her phone and Benj and Alex B. Renner were watching to see what was going to happen next because in about three minutes she was going to be trapped in the corner of the building.

"You better learn this stuff, Joel, in case it's on the driving test."

"There is no written driving test after you get your permit, Eli. You just take a *driving* test, as in a *road test*."

"The guy giving you the road test might ask you some of these questions in case you are ever driving in Kansas or California, so listen."

I grabbed. She sidestepped, retreated, and put the phone behind her back.

"In some towns in California it's illegal to plant rutabagas in roadways or jump from a car at sixty-five miles per hour . . ."

I reached again and missed.

". . . or spill margaritas on the street. And in Oklahoma you can't read comic books while driving. . . ."

Eli was almost all the way to the brick wall by the north entrance of the high school and I said, still grabbing at her phone, "I don't believe you. Let me see it. Just for one minute."

Then Benj was at my side with his phone.

"In Topeka, Kansas, it's illegal to transport dead chickens."

And Eli said, "See?"

Then Benj said, "Joel, you have your own fucking phone. Google this stuff yourself."

And I said, "I can't, asshole. I left my phone in my locker," which wasn't true.

Then Mr. Stanley pulled up and beeped the horn. All the phones were put away and we climbed into the car, and Eli kept slapping at my hands as I was still making moves to grab her phone, which was now in the back pocket of her jeans, and it was just about the most fun I had had in my entire life.

We climbed into the back seat with me on the left and Eli in the middle and Alex B. Renner on the right because according to Mr. Stanley's clipboard it was Benj's turn to get behind the wheel. When we were all seat-belted in the car I was still grabbing at Eli's phone and she was still giggling and Alex B. Renner kept saying, "Cut it out," and Benj turned to Mr. Stanley and said, "In Massachusetts it's illegal to drive with a gorilla in the back seat."

Mr. Stanley just looked at him blankly, his left eye twitching in its typical nervous fashion *di-di-dit dah-dah-dah di-di-dit*, and I was thinking that we each had our own unique way of racking his nerves and Mr. Stanley probably couldn't figure out which one of us upset him more. Benj had some kind of communication problem what with the fact that he blurted out weird stuff all the time and I couldn't drive for shit and Alex B. Renner drove so badly that Mr. Stanley had basically given up trying to correct him and Eli drove so slowly that there were times when I wanted to get out and push the goddamned car and Mr. Stanley had to keep saying, "Eli, if you don't go faster we are going to get rear-ended." Him looking over his shoulder to see the traffic piling up behind us with his eye going *di-di-dit dah-dah-dah di-di-dit,* and me sitting in the back thinking that they should have given the Driver's Ed teacher a gas pedal to go along with the brake pedal for students like Eli, who needed a little coaxing to go faster, but somewhere someone screwed up on that one. Then Benj got all nervous because Mr. Stanley didn't even laugh when he said the gorilla thing, so he added another dose of idiocy to sweeten the pot by blurting out, "In Blairstown, New Jersey, it's illegal to plant trees in the middle of the road," and Mr. Stanley said, "Get out of the driver's seat, Mr. Kutchner, and let Joel drive."

I got in the front seat on the driver's side and Benj got in the back with Eli and Alex B. Renner. I didn't bother to go through Mr. Stanley's preflight checklist of adjusting the mirrors and shit like that that is normally required before we launch this rocket ship, but instead chose to immediately put the car into R for reverse when we were supposed to be going straight ahead in D for drive and then I slammed my foot down hard on the accelerator and we flew backward at high speed. En route, I maneuvered around the Dumpster that was directly behind us, fishtailed, swerved, slammed on the brakes, and then parallel parked perfectly between the janitor's truck and a van from food service without scratching the paint, nicking the side view mirror, *or* damaging the Dumpster. Then I turned the engine off and said, "Ooops. Maybe Eli should drive."

Kutchner said, "Holy shit," Alex B. Renner had gone pale, and Mr.

Stanley said, "I need a minute to collect myself," followed by, "Joel isn't allowed to drive until further notice," and then he took the car keys from me and told me to put on the emergency brake and then he got out of the car and stood all by himself on the side of the parking lot while we waited till he calmed down.

Which, as you might expect, took some time.

While we waited, Benj did one of his what-ifs, asking Eli, "What if you were driving down the highway at twenty-two miles per hour and the rest of the traffic was speeding by you at seventy-five miles per hour? Who would be more likely to get in a crash or get a ticket? One of them or you?" And Eli said, "For as the heavens are higher than the earth, so are my ways higher than your ways and my thoughts than your thoughts."

Which I thought was hysterical because it was basically the good-church-girl way of saying, "Fuck you, Benj."

And Benj said, "Where does she get this shit?"

And Alex B. Renner, who was staring out the car window probably wondering why he was stuck on this planet with us, said, "The Bible. Isaiah 55:9."

Then I said, "Leave her alone."

And Benj said, "I didn't mean nothing by it, I was just wondering. . . ."

Then I asked, "Do you guys think Mr. Stanley is okay?" and all three of them said, "No."

And then Eli got out of the car and went to try to calm him down.

Alex B. Renner said, "I've never seen anyone try so hard or care so much."

I said, "I know, she's like a church."

“What do you think she’s saying to him?” Benj asked as he stared out the car window at them.

“Probably giving him a cake recipe,” I said. “Or maybe she’s just telling him everything on her happy list.”

“Eli has a happy list?”

“Yeah, she adds to it every day at lunch.”

“I wish I had a happy list,” Benj said.

“Me too,” I said.

“So fucking make one,” Alex B. Renner chimed in.

As I looked out the window I was thinking that I wasn’t trying to upset anyone, it was just that it got real boring at times and I hated the driving part of Driver’s Ed and sometimes you had to make your own fun and maybe I was just trying to make Eli feel better, *who the fuck knows*, but nothing was making any sense to me anymore. Not at school, not at the soup kitchen, not with Rooster, not with Eli, not with Mr. Stanley and his goddamned nerves, and not with anything. I had a gun in my garage and Andy wasn’t with me in Driver’s Ed like we planned and I had to remember to feed the Harry Potter mouse and there was a line of hungry people longer than I could see on most Wednesday nights in the greatest country on earth where sometimes people died from friendly fire and that meant that other people couldn’t get jobs because home didn’t feel like home and everyone else was worried about using a comma wrong or who was gay or how to do better on the SATs or how to parallel park and end up less than twelve inches from the curb. And when I started to think about all that I felt my left eye start to twitch *di-di-dit dah-dah-dah di-di-dit* and I rubbed it hard ’cause I didn’t want to end up like old Mr. Stanley, who worried about all the stuff like me and Benj that you can't change anyway. The only good thing that happened was that when Eli came back she asked me to go with her to her church to make peanut butter sandwiches the next day after school.

I asked, "Will Becky be there?"

And Eli said, "Probably."

"And the guy who sings off-key?"

She nodded her head.

"What about the extraterrestrial with the pale blue eyes and the tentacle hands who sucks the ungodly marrow out of you?"

"What?"

"Never mind. But no jelly, right?"

"No jelly."

"Has anyone googled the nutritional value of white bread? Or if peanut butter has trans fats?"

Eli looked genuinely scared.

Then I said that I might still need help in the spreading department and she said that was fine, we could work on it together.

34

WHEN I GOT HOME I HAD TO GO

to Jace's school play with Jackson and Jesus, Mary and it sucked but the good thing was that Jacey didn't wet his pants, which was basically the only thing that I was worried about even though he never wet his pants at school, but still.

After the play we went for an ice-cream cone and Jacey basically made a huge mess but nobody cared.

He was a tree in the play.

A tree with leaves.

Jesus, Mary took lots of pictures and cried.

Jackson said, "Jesus, Mary, it's just a play."

When we got home I sent—didn't send—fourteen text messages to Eli, six to Andy, and three to Principal Redman. The ones to Eli were all about my feelings. The ones to Andy were basically about video games and food in the school cafeteria and the best custom features of Harleys and the ones to Principal Redman were about why juniors should have their own cars (okay, motorcycles) and why I would not be taking the SATs again. Then I told Principal Redman that Mini

Coopers were cool and so were pickup trucks, too, if motorcycles were too dangerous or something. I said that they were all excellent options and then I went to Jace's room to read to him. I got to the chapter in *Winnie-the-Pooh* where Eeyore has a birthday party and gets two presents and Jace fell asleep before I even finished but I kept reading anyway because I wanted to see what happened. Jesus, Mary stopped and stood in the doorway and watched me read for a few minutes and she was holding a bunch of folded laundry and had a look on her face that I had never seen before, like she had waited her whole life for this moment, and had wished that I would read a book to Jace just like I was doing now and if I had known how much it meant to her I would have done it sooner.

When I was finished reading out loud to myself with Jacey asleep next to me I got up and went downstairs and told Jesus, Mary that I was going out, and she said, "Where?" and I said, "Just to walk Lacey," and she looked at me funny 'cause Lacey basically didn't walk anywhere with anyone. When we put her out she normally didn't get too much beyond the front mat unless you gave her a nudge with your foot, but I put the leash on her anyway and took her out, which basically meant that I was walking backward and pulling her forward with me wondering why she couldn't be a more normal dog. Eventually I just tied her leash to the garage door and went inside to check on the gun and maybe text Eli for real or write another desperate, sappy text and then delete it or save it to draft like I had been doing all year. It was like here I was in eleventh grade and the world had gone to shit and I had no real friends and an imaginary girlfriend who I wrote these pathetic text messages to and then didn't send because I always came to my senses.

Sometimes I worried about what would happen if I sent one of the texts by mistake, meaning I typed some stupid, convoluted love text and then went to hit delete or save to draft and then accidentally hit send and then panicked when I heard the *bluuuuurp* sound as my hideous words of love were speeding up to a satellite and then back down to Eli's phone and then I would have to run to her house and break in and hope she was home and demand that she turn over her phone and not look at text messages from Joel and then delete the message myself before she could read it. And then there was the very likely chance that Eli would have been looking right at her phone when I accidently hit send and she would have seen the pathetic text message that would shock her like a zap from a stun gun since she had no idea how I felt about her and then after she recovered from the electric shock she would read it over and over again and then she might tell everyone at school or post it online or start a viral social media post with the hashtag *HilariousLoveTextMessagesFromGuysYouHate*, so basically I tried not to think about that.

Instead I started thinking about how heavy the gun was as I turned it over in my hands and about how it was loaded and that if I pulled the trigger it would change everything and then I remembered that at the soup kitchen this week I noticed Rooster looking at me looking at Eli and I caught his eye and it looked like he almost smiled but maybe not. Then I remembered how Spindini had jumped because there was a loud crash from the kitchen and then he told us about soldiers who have post-traumatic stress disorder—PTSD for short—and he said it could be triggered by a loud noise or a feeling or nothing at all and it was like being scared of monsters that were real once but are no longer there. He basically said, imagine that you're driving in your car or riding on a bus right here in this town maybe up on West Main or Kennedy Boulevard near the senior center and the Boys & Girls Club of America and all of a sudden you have a flashback and you think that you are back in Afghanistan or Iraq in Kandahar or Mosul getting ready to mount up and move out on a Hell Train mission and then just like that with no warning the sat phones are down and enemy soldiers are firing at you and it is as real as when it was real and you can't differentiate between being at war and being here on a bus or driving in your car and it's like now there's a virtual-reality war game playing in your head that turns on all by itself like a TV you have no control over or a video game that is way realer than any game you have ever played. He said that it starts at level six-to-the-tenth power and plays over and over again and won't stop and in this game you would see your best friend get shot in the chest over and over again and you would see his face knowing that this is it, and then you would try again and again to save him and you think that this time you won't stop trying to stop the bleeding just like you didn't stop trying to stop the bleeding in Kandahar or Fallujah or Mosul or Baghdad but then you can't get it to stop now just like you couldn't get it to stop then because sometimes the holes that bullets put in people are so big that you just can't stop all the bleeding no matter how hard you try.

Then he told us that more than 250,000 veterans who have returned from Iraq and Afghanistan have PTSD and when you include vets from all the wars, not just Afghanistan and Iraq, 22 vets a day commit suicide. He said that some people argue that that number overstates the problem but then he said, "That's bullshit. Even if it's one vet committing suicide it's too many." Then he added, "That's why I didn't do well as a plumber because I would see my buddy dying over and over again and be thinking about killing myself and not be able to fix somebody's sink while that was going on." Then he said that seeing a buddy die was the worst thing that could happen to you in war. It was even worse than killing someone or dying yourself. Then I asked him to repeat that and he said, "Seeing a buddy die is the worst thing that could happen to you in war. It is even worse than killing someone or dying yourself."

Then I got up and went over to Rooster and leaned in close and said, "Do you think you have PTSD?" And Rooster held up one finger for yes, and then he got up and left and after he was gone I whispered to myself, "I think I do, too."

Later Eli sent me a text that said:

I can't show you what more than 250,000 vets with PTSD look like, but this is what the 22 vets a day who commit suicide look like:

And then repeat that every single day of the year.
And every single year.

I was still sitting in the garage holding the gun and now I was thinking about that many soldiers and feeling really sad and then I texted Eli *I love you I love you I love you I love you I love you* and then hit save to draft and didn't hear an accidental bluuuurp, which was a good thing based on the scenario I had just gone through in my head.

Then I texted her, *Seeing a buddy die is the worst thing that could happen to you in war. It is even worse than killing someone or dying yourself,* and saved that text to draft, too. Then I put the gun away and walked back to the house.

We got measured and weighed in gym today. Kutchner grew two inches; Alex B. Renner grew two and a half inches. And I was one quarter of an inch shorter and four pounds lighter than I was in September.

I had them check three times.

That just didn't seem fair.

The world was getting bigger and I was shrinking.

TEXT FROM JOEL TO ANDY 12:57 p.m.

Jacey doesn't have Rocky Mountain spotted fever anymore. His rash is gone but I have PTSD, ADD, GERD, IBS, RLS, and all kinds of other shit too.
And that's just this week.
My mom said I should stay off WebMD.
I said no fucking way.
Just without the fucking part and the no part.
I pretty much said okay I'll try.

TEXT FROM JOEL TO PRINCIPAL REDMAN 1:04 a.m.

Just having a gun makes me think of things that I would never have thought of before, because it feels like the gun gives me the power to fix things.
Like it makes me more right and smarter or taller even.
Which makes no sense at all because having the gun just makes everything worse. But it's just fucking true anyway because that's how it makes me feel.

Sorry I said fucking.

TEXT FROM JOEL TO PRINCIPAL REDMAN 1:14 a.m.

One of the vets at the soup kitchen told me that he has a lot of guns in his apartment. Handguns and rifles and extra ammo.
He said it makes him feel safe.
Like he could protect himself if he had to.
He doesn't have a job or food. He has guns.

TEXT FROM JOEL TO PRINCIPAL REDMAN 1:24 a.m.

I think I have PTSD. That's when your brain is messed up because you suffered something too upsetting to get better from.

The vet at the soup kitchen with all the guns told me that when you have PTSD you can have flashbacks and keep reliving the thing that's too awful to think about that traumatized you.

If that's true, I have PTSD. Just so you know.
Because of Andy.
You remember Andy, don't you?

THE NEXT DAY AT SCHOOL

I was standing in front of my locker putting some books away and Eli walked over and said, "Do you think we could do it again?"

I looked up. "What do you mean?"

"Do you think we can steal some eggs and asparagus?"

"Did you say *steal*?"

"Maybe."

"I think you said steal." I called out into the hallway, "Eli said steal!"

"So what if I did, Joel?" Then she leaned in and whispered, "I read on the internet that *almost half* of the food produced in this county either gets thrown away or rots in the farmers' fields or ends up in the trash behind supermarkets and restaurants and in people's kitchens. The way I figure it, that's a crime against humanity way worse than stealing food that no one is going to eat."

"Eli, I believe I've corrupted you."

"Maybe just a little, teeny-weeny bit, Higgins. Okay, so on Wednesday we can go steal some eggs?"

"Hell, yes."

"And asparagus."

"And asparagus."

"You'll bring the camo?"

"I'll bring the camo."

"Do you have access to any other farms?"

"No, I do not!" I put my jacket in my locker and slammed it closed. "But if you want we can rob the ShopRite over on Route 112."

"Joel!" She shook her head and walked away.

I called after her, "Or, how about the minimart at the Mobil station? Or Starbucks? We'll break in the front window and steal all the Krispy Kremes."

She was probably thinking that *Joel is such an abomination*, but even as I watched her from behind, I could tell she was smiling.

TEXT FROM JOEL TO ANDY 12:24 a.m.

I was thinking that I might ask Eli on a date.

But maybe I should wait until I get my driver's license.

I can't ask her to walk somewhere. Can I?

TEXT FROM JOEL TO PRINCIPAL REDMAN 12:42 a.m.

It's me. Joel Higgins again. A couple of things. We should approach the town because everywhere I look I see places we could grow food. Like by the stop signs and in the median strips between the lanes on the highway. And in the field next to the library and up on West Main or on Kennedy Boulevard by the Boys & Girls Club.

And we could keep chickens in the boys'
locker room, not just the gym.
I mean, come on. We won't need the locker room
for changing if the gym is full of chickens.

36

TEXT FROM JESUS, MARY TO JOEL 2:17 p.m.

WE NEED TO TALK COME HOME RIGHT NOW.

Oh shit!

The thing was, I didn't know if she found the gun or the mouse.

Or which would be worse.

Probably the gun.

Definitely the gun.

TEXT FROM JESUS, MARY TO JOEL 3:15 p.m.

WHERE R U????

TEXT FROM JOEL TO JESUS, MARY 3:17 P.M.

At church with Eli making peanut butter sandwiches for the homeless.

TEXT FROM JESUS, MARY TO JOEL 3:18 p.m.

Come home NOW!

TEXT FROM JOEL TO JESUS, MARY 3:18 P.M.

People will be hungry, then.

TEXT FROM JESUS, MARY TO JOEL 3:19 p.m.

I DON'T CARE!

TEXT FROM JESUS, MARY TO JOEL 3:27 p.m.

JOEL IT IS ME JACEY

MOM FOOND THE MONNSTERR

37

JESUS, MARY SCREAMED SO LOUD

that the police came to the house.

Mrs. Faust next door heard "a bloodcurdling cry" and immediately called 911 to report a scream "indicative of a homicide at 257 Barker Street." She should have said *I want to report a loud scream that could be indicative of anything, like my neighbor has a five-year-old who is keeping Harry Potter's mouse in a box in his closet and it scared the crap out of his mother when she saw it as she was putting his toys away.* But she went with full-on overreact.

The police thought it was funny.

I found out later that Officer Jim Hannity called Jackson on his cell phone 'cause he had the number because they knew each other from high school and played together on a summer softball team for men over forty, and he was laughing his head off and said, "Your wife's got a hell of a set of lungs."

Jackson said, "What's that supposed to mean?"

And Hannity said, "You better call an exterminator. Mary saw a mouse and screamed so loud the lady next door had a heart attack."

Not really, but they took Mrs. Faust to the hospital for observation because she was eighty-seven years old and she got all shook up.

Jesus, Mary was not happy with me for a whole lot of complicated reasons.

For starters, disease.

"Do you understand that the mouse you caught is a bacteria-ridden rodent?"

And I said, "Now I know where I get my hypochondria, Mom."

She said, "I'm really disappointed here, boys."

I said, "But . . ."

And Jesus, Mary said, "Don't interrupt with a 'but,' Joel. There is no 'but' here. And don't be fresh with me."

And I said, "I wasn't being fresh. Why does everyone think that I'm being fresh when I'm not?"

Jacey said, "Are you going to kill Scabbers?"

Jesus, Mary said, "Of course not," and she rubbed his head.

I said, "What about all the diseases you can't catch from a mouse?"

Jesus, Mary said, "*Whaaat??*"

And then she said, "Both of you go wash your hands a thousand times."

Jacey said, "But I didn't even touch him!"

"I don't care. Plus, your father will be here in a minute."

I said, "Mom, you didn't have to call Jackson over a little mouse."

And Jesus, Mary said she didn't call Jackson, the police did when Mrs. Faust next door heard the scream and thought there was a murder and had to be taken to the hospital because of angina.

And then I said, "Oh, shit! Are you serious?"

And Jesus, Mary said, "You're damned right I'm serious."

Jacey said, "Potty mouth! Both of you! Potty mouth!"

And then it calmed down and me and Jace washed our hands and it got quiet except for the mouse scratching noises and then Jace said, "It's not a *little* mouse, Joel. It's Scabbers!" And then he added, "And don't be mad, Mom, it was a secret brother project and Joel caught the monster in my closet."

Jesus, Mary calmed down and kissed Jacey's head but then she got riled up again and pulled out her phone and said, "Here are all the possible disease vectors and routes of contamination," and I said, "Seriously, Mom? Disease vectors and routes of contamination? You have to stop reading so much WebMD," and she gave me a look. "It's not good for you, so hand over your phone," I added.

She didn't.

Instead she launched into another rant about the horrors of handling infected animal carcasses and breathing in bacteria and dust that's contaminated with rodent urine or droppings and the dire implications of direct contact with rodents and their urine and droppings and of course the deadly health consequences of eating food that is contaminated with rodent urine or droppings. Jacey said, "What's droppings?" and I said, "Poop," and he said, "Why would I eat poop?" And it basically went downhill from there.

In a nutshell here was Jacey's defense: He didn't handle any carcasses, Scabbers takes lots of baths, he never put his food in Scabbers's box, he would never eat dog kibble, and Joel is in charge of poop and pee. That last one he kept repeating.

Then Jackson's truck pulled up the driveway and he came upstairs to the scene of the crime and listened to everyone's side and then he said, "Jesus, Mary, you didn't have to scream so loud that you gave Margaret angina over a mouse!"

Jacey said, "We shouldn't be talking about Mrs. Faust's vagina."

We all looked momentarily confused, and then Jackson quickly said, "I agree," and everyone but Jace laughed.

And then Jackson said, "Okay, boys. Pack up Scabbers and bring him to the truck."

Jacey said, "No way!"

Jackson said, "Way!"

Then Jacey said, "Joel, do something!"

I picked up Scabbers's box and headed to the truck.

JACKSON TOLD JACE

that a mouse's favorite place in the world to live was on top of a big heap of garbage.

It was a hard statement to disagree with.

Jacey was sitting on the bench seat in the front of the truck in between Jackson and me and he had Scabbers on his lap in his little box and Jackson let Jace shift the gears a few times to distract him so he wouldn't cry.

When we pulled into the county waste center, Jackson said he knew the guy manning the gate and told us his name was Fred Haze and he drove a '97 Dodge Ram with a finicky transmission. After Jackson told Fred that he had to drop some trash off Jacey said, "Scabbers isn't trash," and Fred said he had to weigh the truck coming in and going out and Jackson laughed on account of the fact that the only thing we were dropping off was Scabbers and he knew how much he weighed. Jackson explained to Jace that was how they figured out how much to charge and that it's two hundred bucks a ton and Jacey said, "Does Scabbers weigh a ton?" And Jackson said, "A ton is two thousand pounds. Do you think a mouse could weigh two thousand pounds?" And Jacey said, "Maybe." And then we set him free—Scabbers, not Jacey—on the biggest pile of trash you have ever seen. The little guy scrambled way up onto the top of the heap and picked up a banana peel and Jackson said, "See?"

The three of us had a *Free Willy* moment up at the garbage dump. So it wasn't as bad as you might think.

On the way out Jacey was drawing a picture of Scabbers with a crayon and paper he found in the glove box of the pickup and in it Scabbers was sitting on top of heaps of trash with a whole bunch of other mice. When we got to the gate, Fred weighed the truck again and said, "That will be forty bucks." And Jackson said, "No way!" and Jacey said, "Way!"

And then Fred said, "Only kidding, Jackson, no charge. Get the hell out of here."

And Jacey said, "Potty mouth!"

Late that night Jace came into my room and climbed into my top bunk and said, "We're gonna need that other trap, Joel. The monsters are back."

ME AND ELI WENT TO THE RICHARDSONS' FARM AGAIN

a few days later and on the bus ride over I told her that we have several choices: an omelet with asparagus; pasta with cream, nutmeg, and asparagus; or a frittata.

She burst out laughing. "Joel, what on earth is a frittata?"

"I have absolutely no idea."

"But you know how to cook?"

"That would be a hard no."

"But you like feeding people?"

"Yes. I like feeding people. But that doesn't mean that I believe in God."

"I didn't ask you if you believed in God. I just asked you if you liked to cook."

"And feed people."

"And feed people."

We were sitting on the bus together wearing matching camouflage. Our fingers were next to each other on the seat, practically touching. I almost reached for her hand a thousand times but didn't. I mean, it was only a finger stretch away. It would have been so easy but it was the hardest thing in the world to pull the trigger on. Then just when I was about to make a move, she lifted her hand to brush the hair off of her face.

I started to sweat like the Pittster.

Retreated to my side of the seat.

Almost passed out.

Eli said, "Joel, are you feeling okay?"

I said, "Fuck no, I'm not feeling the least bit okay. In fact, I'm about to barf. I've sweated through my clothes because I want to hold your hand but I feel like if I try, it might ruin everything."

Just without the "Fuck no." And the part about "I'm not feeling the least bit okay." And minus the bit about me being "about to barf." And the bit about "sweating through my clothes." And the part about wanting to hold her hand. And I also left off the last thing about how if I did, it might ruin everything.

So I pretty much said, "Sure thing, why do you ask?"

"No reason."

Painful awkward silence, at least on my part, then Eli said, "You still coming with me tomorrow to make sandwiches over in the church basement?"

I said, "Maybe we should make frittatas instead."

"You're having trouble with peanut butter sandwiches, so frittatas, whatever they are, are a definite no."

Then the bus stopped at the corner of Main and Lexington and we got off and headed up the hill in silence. When we got to the farm we cut in on the same path as before and I purposely skirted Rooster's place again, praying that we didn't bump into him by accident.

Then as soon as we saw the chicken coop, Eli got all enthusiastic and ran ahead into the building and started collecting eggs like it was the most fun she'd ever had in her whole life. After we had collected six full crates of eggs and I was about to say we should move on, I looked up and froze. Mr. Miller, the guy from the hardware store, was standing in the doorway.

Eli looked up a second later and she froze, too.

The three of us looked at each other for a long minute without saying a thing and then Mr. Miller just nodded his head and walked off.

Eli turned to me and whispered, "Do you know who that was?"

I whispered back, "Yes."

She asked, "Who?"

And I said, "God." And I made sure not to laugh.

Eli looked from me to the door where Mr. Miller had been standing in silhouette as the light was pouring in making it look all heavenly, but he was nowhere to be seen. She looked back at me and said, "Joel Higgins, God is not a farmer."

I said, "How do you know?"

And she said absolutely nothing. Both of us just stood there staring at the henhouse door.

Then, with all the beautiful light pouring in and the chickens running around at our feet clucking, I asked, "What do you think happens when you die?"

Eli was silent for a minute but then she said, "You are overcome with radiant warmth and engulfed in light and peace and you live for eternity in the embrace of God's love."

"So that's what happens to all the soldiers who die and all the kids with cancer and—"

"Yes."

"And you really believe that?"

"I do."

As I looked back toward the doorway I was thinking that I really wished that I could believe that, too.

Then I said, "Let's go pick asparagus."

And she said, "Joel, what should we say if we bump into . . ."

"God?"

"Not God. *Him*," she answered as she gestured toward the door.

I thought for a moment and then said, "Either way, God or not God, I'd go with 'hi.'"

That night, after we served the poached eggs on top of the asparagus at the soup kitchen and were about to close up, I asked Spindini if he believed in God and he said, "Yes."

So then I asked him, "Even with all the death and killing in war?" and he said, "Especially with all the death and killing in war."

Then he said, "If there's no God then that means that we're all alone and this is it." Then he just shook his head and said that he couldn't face that because that would mean that all his buddies were just gone.

I stood up. Stepped back, knocked a chair over by accident, and said, "You're definitely right, then. There is a God." And I walked over to Eli and said, "The whole God thing?"

"Yes?"

"I've been thinking about it and I'm a bit more flexible."

And she said, "That's good to know, Joel. But that guy at the farm today was not Him."

And I said, "Eli, I know that. I was just messing with you."

TEXT FROM JOEL TO ELI 11:06 p.m.

I saw you praying once. You were kneeling at the casket.

Andy's casket.

You looked so beautiful.

Your hands were folded and your head was down

and your lips were moving and you looked so calm. I

thought, I want that. What Eli has. I really do.

TEXT FROM JOEL TO ANDY 11:12 p.m.

Where are you?

40

TEXT FROM ELI TO JOEL 12:35 a.m.

Joel R U up?

TEXT FROM JOEL TO ELI 12:37 a.m.

Always. Never sleep. What up?

TEXT FROM ELI TO JOEL 12:38 a.m.

Can you go get Benj? He's drunk.

TEXT FROM JOEL TO ELI 12:38 a.m.

How do you know?

TEXT FROM ELI TO JOEL 12:39 a.m.

He texted A. J. and A. J. texted me and he said, GET JOEL TO GET HIM.

TEXT FROM JOEL TO ELI 12:39 a.m.

Where is he?

TEXT FROM ELI TO JOEL 12:40 a.m.

In front of the soup kitchen throwing up.

TEXT FROM JOEL TO ELI 12:43 A.M.

Can't he call someone else??

TEXT FROM ELI TO JOEL 12:44 a.m.

He has no friends.

TEXT FROM JOEL TO ELI 12:46 A.M.

What about his aunt?

TEXT FROM ELI TO JOEL 12:47 a.m.

He said he would rather die.

TEXT FROM JOEL TO ELI 12:47 A.M.

Fuck!

TEXT FROM ELI TO JOEL 12:49 a.m.

Joel!!!

TEXT FROM JOEL TO ELI 12:49 A.M.

Fine. I'll do it.

41

"KNOCK, KNOCK . . ."

"Who's there?"

"It's Joel."

"Joel who?"

"Very funny, Mom. Can I come in?"

"It's almost one a.m. Is something wrong?"

I opened the door a crack. Jesus, Mary was leaning up on her elbow squinting at me. Jackson was holding a pillow over his head.

"You know how you said that if I ever needed help you would be there no questions asked?"

Jesus, Mary switched on the lamp next to the bed and Jackson sat up shielding his eyes from the light and looked at me.

"Yes."

"Did you mean it?"

Jackson said, "Probably not," but Jesus, Mary smacked him and said, "Of course we did."

"Can you drive me somewhere? No questions asked? It's important."

"Now?" she asked.

"Now."

Jackson said, "I'll do it. Come on, Joel, get some shoes on. Pants might be a good idea, too."

By the time I put on pants and pulled a sweatshirt over my head and grabbed my shoes, Jackson was sitting in the truck with the engine running. When I climbed in he was smoking a cigarette and he said, "Don't tell your mom." And then added, "Don't ever smoke." Then he popped the truck into reverse and backed down the driveway and said, "Where to?"

"Hendricks and Main."

"We're not going to rob the donut store or the fix-it shop, are we?"

"No, Pop. We're just gonna pick up a drunk kid."

"One of your friends?"

I was looking out the window at the houses on our street and there were no lights on at all except for at the Andersons' place and Jackson always said they must get free electricity or something 'cause they never turned any of their lights out. Not even their outdoor Christmas lights, which they kept turned on all year, even in the summer, and they were the twinkly kind that made their house look like there was always some kind of party going on. And then I wiped the steam off the inside of the window and said, "You know that I don't have any friends anymore."

It was quiet for a few minutes after that and then Jackson said, "Okay, well, where are we taking this drunk person who is not your friend after we pick him up at one thirty in the morning?"

"Home."

"As in *his* home or *our* home?"

"Our home."

"Doesn't he have a home?"

"Nope."

"Okay, then. Our home it is."

"No questions, right?"

"Only one."

"Fuck."

"No potty mouth."

"So what's your question?"

"Does this drunk kid who's not your friend like the Yankees? 'Cause if he doesn't like the Yankees . . ."

I rolled my eyes and said, "Just drive, please. And thanks, Pop."

Then Jackson said, "This drunk kid we're picking up, it isn't a girl, is it?"

"Unfortunately not."

42

I FOUND BENJ

just as Eli had promised, sitting on the curb in front of the soup kitchen with his shoes covered in vomit.

I texted Eli, *Got him.*

She texted back, *thks!*

Benj looked up at me and said, "Joel?"

"Yep. Come on, let's go."

"Joel?"

"Hop up. We're going to drive you to my house."

"I don't feel so good."

"I'll bet."

"Can I ask you something?" He was slurring his speech.

"No. Just get up and get in the truck."

Benj got up and staggered to the truck and Jackson got out of the cab to size up the situation.

Jackson leaned in close to me and whispered, "Isn't that Benj Kutchner? The kid you hit?"

"Jackson meet Benj. Benj, Jackson."

Jackson said, "Put him in the back, Joel. And you sit with him. Here. Use this in case he throws up again." Then he handed me a garbage bag.

"Is this your dad, Joel?"

"No, Benj. He's just some stranger I found in the middle of the night who was willing to come pick you up."

"Hi, Joel's dad."

"Jesus, Joel, get him to take his shoes off. We'll toss them in the back. I'll wait for you in the truck."

"Okay, here's the thing . . ." Benj said.

"Benj, please just take your sneakers off and get in the truck."

He almost fell.

"Maybe you better sit down to take your shoes off."

Benj replied, "Nope. I can do it standing up."

I had the back door to the cab open and was standing behind Benj trying to block him as he stumbled backward. It took a while but he eventually got one lace undone.

"Here's the thing. . . . What if . . ."

"Benj, stop! Just stop talking. Sit down and take your shoes off and then get in the truck. No what-ifs. . . ."

He kept stumbling backward as he was trying to untie his other sneaker. Then he almost fell flat on his face several times, but I kept catching him under the arms and kind of propping him back up on his feet.

"What if you're fifteen years old and your parents are driving late at night on . . . What's the name of that big highway that goes all the way from Florida to Maine?" And Jackson called out, "I-95," from the truck and Benj said, "That's the one, I-95." Then he said, "So if they're driving north between Baltimore and Philly on I-95 because they were at an orthodontist convention and—"

"Benj, not now."

"—and your dad is driving and right in front of him just past a bridge overpass there's a barricade due to road construction and there's a jackknifed tractor trailer just around the bend but he doesn't know that yet and there's a fucking eighteen-wheeler loaded with gasoline barreling down from behind him, and the driver of that truck had been driving for twenty-three hours straight and your dad doesn't know that either . . ."

Benj now had one sneaker completely off.

". . . and your dad tries to swerve around the barricade and your mom is sitting in the front seat next to him knitting a sweater and they are probably just listening to the radio—WPIX Jazz Top 40, maybe—and talking about summer vacation like you always take to the shore and they have no idea that there won't be a summer vacation or a summer and they have no idea what is about to happen . . ."

Then Benj threw up. And I mean a river. Then he wiped the back of his hand across his mouth, finally got the second sneaker off and then continued in a rambling drunken slur.

". . . then what if your dad sideswipes the tractor trailer and almost recovers control of the car but then his car gets flattened by the eighteen-wheeler full of gasoline that came up from behind him with the driver who hadn't slept for a whole day but stayed awake by popping amphetamines . . ."

And then Benj just stopped talking and looked straight ahead and I thought, *Say something, Joel.*

". . . and then your parents' car bursts into flames in a fireball that could be seen for miles around because it exploded on impact . . ."

Benj was waving his arms around like a bomb had gone off.

". . . and then what if that happens and you don't have any brothers or sisters and you have to move in with your aunt who you don't even hardly know and she doesn't have a husband or kids, so it's just two strangers living together because they have to and then you show up at a new school where everyone thinks that you are . . ."

He throws up again.

". . . and you don't have any friends and—"

"Benj, I'm your friend."

"You don't even like me, Joel." He was crying now.

"Yes, I do."

"No, you don't."

Then Benj started to cry more and I was still thinking, *Say something! Anything at all, Joel!*

"Okay, here's a what-if, Benj. What if your best friend from kindergarten who you hung out with all the time and all summer every summer and every day after school got acute lymphoblastic leukemia last year and you still spent every afternoon with him even when he couldn't go to school because he was so sick from chemo and cancerous blood cells were boxing out his healthy blood cells and that meant that he couldn't get oxygen or clot anymore and you watched as he went from sick to sicker to too sick to almost dead and his hair fell out and he got so pale you could see through him like he was disappearing and he threw up every day all day and he lost so much weight you couldn't look at him but you had to look at him because he was your best friend."

I stopped talking and Benj was just looking at me waiting for me to finish so I said, "And you didn't want him to know that you felt guilty all the time because every once in a while you had fun at lunch or saw a movie or got a hamburger and didn't even think about him once the whole time even though he was dying. And then what if he told you that he didn't want to live anymore and that he was only breathing today because he didn't want his mom to be sadder than she was right now and then you show up one day and his mom answers the door and she says, 'Joel, he's gone,' and you say, 'Gone? What do you mean, Mrs. Westfield? Andy can't be gone . . .' because even though you knew this was coming somehow you still thought it wasn't."

Benj was just staring at me now like he was seeing me as someone who had the same disease that he had.

Then Benj said, "I think I'm going to throw up again."

I said, "Me too."

"You're not even drunk, Joel."

"I know."

And then Benj barfed and I barfed all over the side of the road and Jackson climbed out of the truck and put his hands on our shoulders and said, "Come on, boys, let's go home."

43

AFTER WE GOT HOME AND I GOT BENJ UPSTAIRS,

I walked out to the garage, pulled open the door, and then made my way to the back wall by the pile of old bricks Jackson had stacked up.

I knelt down, counted three bricks to the left and four down, then pulled two bricks out, slipped the gun out from its hiding place, removed it from the plastic bag, and carefully unwrapped it from the rag. Then I sat down on the ledge that jutted out from the wall and placed the gun in my lap. It was almost 3:00 a.m. and pitch dark and it had started to rain hard and the rain was pounding down on the roof as I pulled my cell phone out from my sweatshirt pocket, then tapped the phone icon, hit voice mail, put it on speaker, and hit play. I'd done this a thousand times since last summer; I played the only saved voice message I had.

Hey, man. Are you coming over? I missed you yesterday.

I hit pause. Went back to the beginning. Then hit play to listen to the message again. My hands were shaking.

Hey, man. Are you coming over? I missed you yesterday.

Pause. Went back a little. Hit play.

I missed you yesterday. And the day before. Don't give up on me.

I hit pause, went back a few seconds again. The tears were coming.

Don't give up on me. You're all that I have.

Went back. Hit play.

You're all that I have.

Went back. Then play again.

You're all that I have. I hope they had pizza for lunch and chocolate milk. And pretzels.

I put the phone down, picked up the gun, and stood up. Held the gun out in front of me. At arm's length.

A shooter's stance.

My muscles trembled and my finger on the trigger of the gun twitched. I aimed straight at the garage door like I was going to fire. Moved my line of sight a few inches to the left. Took aim at an old paint bucket, then at the tractor, then at an old broken flowerpot. I wiped the tears from the corners of my eyes with my shirtsleeve. I was Spindini in the wheel well of a Humvee with my last round chambered so I wouldn't be taken alive trying like hell to honor the creed that no man is left behind. *I was ready to shoot at anything that fucking moved.* In that moment everything in my life looked like an enemy that needed to be taken down. It's fucking hard to be a normal kid and go to school and learn algebra and take the SATs when your friend dies and you can't find your way back home. Even when the voice mail wasn't playing, I could still hear Andy's words.

Hey, man. Are you coming over?

I missed you yesterday. And the day before. Don't give up on me.

They were like bombs going off in my head.

You're all that I have.

I sat back down trembling and sweating. I put the gun back in my lap. Picked up my phone again. Played the message so I could hear Andy's voice for real. I wanted to feel the pain.

They

were

violent

words

and there

was

no

safe

place

to

hide

from

them.

Hey, man. Are you coming over? I missed you yesterday. And the day before. Don't give up on me. You're all that I have. I hope they had pizza for lunch and chocolate milk. And pretzels.

Andy sounded upbeat, happy even. Not like someone who was abandoned by his best friend when he was going to die in two fucking days.

How come he had to die in two days?

Andy could have at least sounded pissed off. That would have been way better than this. I yelled into the dark of the garage, "You should have said, *What the fuck, man? You're my best friend and you won't even stop by to see me before I fucking die? Don't leave me behind!*"

Those words split the air around me.

Hit an artery.

I bled out. Didn't bleed out. Wished I bled out. Looked around for a tourniquet. Couldn't find one.

Doesn't he see? It was friendly fire. I didn't mean anything by it.

I didn't know he was going to die in two days.

I should have known he was going to die in two days.

I whispered in the dead, dark air of the garage, "I'm not coming over anymore, Andy. Not ever. And I'm sorry. So sorry."

I whispered as the rain pounded down on the roof, "They had pizza for lunch and chocolate milk and pretzels that day, Andy." I was still shaking. Sobbing.

I texted Eli: *There is no God.*

Then I hit delete.

Texted her again: *There has to be a God. For Spindini. And Andy. And . . .*

Hit save to draft, then got up.

Dropped my phone back into my pocket, then kicked the side of an empty gas can and sent it flying.

Then I shut my phone off.

My hands were still shaking.

I took the bullet out of the chamber, wrapped the gun back up in the rag, and put it back in its hiding place, tucked it underneath and inside the stack of bricks. Four bricks down from the top. Three over to the left.

On my way out of the garage I was skittish and jumpy. I heard Spindini's voice play back in my head, *no man left behind . . . seeing your buddy die is even worse than killing someone or dying yourself. . . .* I stumbled in the dark, tripped over a paint can, then stopped to pick up a small blue Matchbox police car that was lying on the cement near the trash bins by the garage doors and put it in my pocket to give back to Jace. It was pitch-black outside because I hadn't flipped on the outside lights, so I lost my footing a couple of times as I staggered back to the house in the driving rain drunk with pain. I was thinking about the fact that in Driver's Ed today when I put the car in R for reverse when I was supposed to be in D for drive to mess with Mr. Stanley again, he grabbed my arm and said, "Joel, at some point you are going to have to stop going backward and put the vehicle in drive and move forward." He put a big emphasis on the word *forward*.

And I knew he was right.

But Andy was back there, and I didn't know what was up ahead.

When I stepped inside the house through the front door Jackson looked up from the TV and I managed to say, "What are you still doing up, Pop?"

"Couldn't sleep. I taped last week's game in Cleveland, so I decided to watch it."

I took off my sneakers and he asked, "What were you doing outside in the rain at this hour?" His voice was soft, un-Jackson-like.

I just looked at him like he was speaking a language I didn't understand, then mumbled, "I was just checking email. There's better cell service out in the garage."

Jackson sat back in his chair. It was going on 4:00 a.m. He took a swig from the beer can he was holding but didn't bother challenging me. Instead he said, "The damn game got delayed 'cause of rain and the goddamned Yanks were up by six runs."

I said, "Maybe that's just God's way of punishing you." And Jackson did a double take and then looked at me long and hard before he said, "Jesus, Joel. God's got better things to do than punish me by raining out the Yankee game."

I looked at him.

Then Jackson said, "I'm so sorry about Andy, son. I really am."

And I said, "Don't worry, the Yanks have a good chance at the pennant this year, Dad. You'll see."

And he said, "Joel . . ."

And I said, "Good night, Pop."

And he said, "Joel."

And I said, "I can't."

44

BENJ ENDED UP STAYING WITH US

for a few days.

He slept in the top bunk and I slept in the bottom bunk, which meant that when Jace came in because he wet his bed I had to put him in the bottom bunk and I had to go sleep on the couch 'cause I wasn't going to change his sheets in the middle of the night or argue with him. In the morning when Jesus, Mary would come downstairs she would say, "Joel, what are you doing down here?" And I would say, "Your whole plan about ignoring the bed wetting isn't working 'cause the only thing getting extinguished is my privacy." And Jesus, Mary would say something like, "Oh, sorry, honey! Did Jace show up in your room again last night?"

And I'd be thinking, *What's wrong with her? Probably Alzheimer's or dementia or some other early stage cognitive degenerative disease.*

Then Benj and Jace would come thundering down the stairs and they would be playing What if. . . .

Benj would say something dumb like, "What if there was a gorilla in the kitchen and you had to get him out?" And Jacey would say, "That's easy, I would just use Gorilla Glue to stick him to the floor and then I would hit him with my Wiffle ball bat and then he would go zonk! And then I would eat pancakes and watch TV!"

Then Benj would say, "Well, what if the Gorilla Glue didn't work and he lifted his big gorilla arms . . ." and then Benj would lift his big gorilla arms and start to roar and then they would be running around the house playing Angry Gorilla and Jackson would come down the stairs and say, "What the hell is all this racket?" And Benj would say, "Potty mouth! Mr. Higgins has a potty mouth!" And Jacey would laugh and laugh. And then Jackson would come into the kitchen and say, "Tell me when we can send Benj home." And I would say, "Not yet, Pop," and he would say, "Okay, Joel."

And then, a few days later, Benj announced that he was ready to go back to his aunt's house.

At dinner the night after we took Benj home, Jackson said, "Hey, Joel, I didn't want to say anything with Kutchner here but three wrecks came into the shop a few days ago."

Jackson told us that the insurance company was jammed up because of tornadoes in Indiana and the adjuster couldn't come look at the cars for at least another week to do an estimate but they were totaled anyway. "Still drive, though," he said, and I knew what he was thinking.

We exchanged a look.

"How about crash-car combat, Joel?"

I smiled.

Crash-car combat was when Jackson and me would take wrecked cars that were going to be picked up by the car-crushing company after the insurance companies had declared them totaled—or sometimes right before that—and we would bring them in the middle of the night on Jackson's flatbed to a parking field up by the go-cart track that was owned by Hugh Jenson, the fire chief, who sometimes conducted drills with the wrecks to teach firefighters how to put out car fires. But anyway, we wrecked the cars even more. Just hauled off and crashed them into each other like a demolition derby or monster truck rally.

"Wait, I have another idea," I said. "You say there are three and they all drive?"

"Yup."

"Can you tow them to the lot?"

"But we're not going to crash them?" Jackson asked, disappointed.

Jesus, Mary said, "Jackson, you sound like Jace!"

"Oh, I'm gonna crash them, just not with you," I said.

"And why is that?"

"I want to use them to teach Eli how to parallel park."

"Eli? That cute little girl who sang that awful song at Family Fun Night at Shady Brook?"

Jesus, Mary said, "She's not so little anymore, Jackson."

"But she's still pretty," Jacey said. "I see her waiting for the bus sometimes when we pick up Joel."

Jacey was crashing trucks together on the dinner table right next to his plate, which he wasn't supposed to be doing, so I said, "No trucks at the table, Jace," and he said, "No 'lectronics at the dinner table, Joel!" I swiped my phone off the table and stuck it in my pocket and he swiped his trucks off the table and stuck them in his pocket and then I stuck my tongue out at him and he said, "You tattled first!" And Jackson said, "Do you two want to take this outside?" and Jacey said, "We're not evenly matched. I'd take him in a second," and Jesus, Mary said, "Eat your string beans, Jace," and he said, "I did," and I said, "They're in his pocket," and he got mad and crossed his arms in a huff and then he started to hold his breath and then I tickled him and when he was wiggling a couple of the string beans fell out of his pocket and onto the floor and he said, "I was going to eat them later!" and Jackson said, "I can't stand this commotion. I'm taking my food in by the game."

Then Jacey said, "Ha-ha, Jackson, you'll miss all the fun."

Jackson hated when Jacey called him by his name but he didn't say anything about it this time. He just smiled at Jesus, Mary and said, "I'll take my chances on that." But before he left he turned to me and said, "Is this driving lesson tomorrow with Eli by any chance a date?"

And I said, "Sadly no, Pop. It's just that Mr. Stanley said that no one else gets to drive until Eli can parallel park and it's been two weeks and there is no chance in hell that even if we spend the rest of our lives trying to parallel park with her behind the wheel that—"

"Got it, son. Extreme measures."

"Yes, sir. Extreme measures."

45

"WILL YOUR DAD BE THERE?"

Eli asked when we were standing next to our lockers and I told her about the parking plan.

I took her asking about my dad as a good sign because she didn't give me an Auto No, which, when it came to girls, was sort of like an Auto F.

I said, "My dad will just drop us off and then he'll leave us there until I call him to pick us up. Which, by the way, won't be until you can park like a valet."

"And you really think that you can teach me how to parallel park?"

Eli had disbelief plastered on her face and her hand on her hip like she always did when she was thinking that I was somehow trying to pull one over on her.

"I *know* I can teach you how to parallel park."

Which wasn't completely true. I mean, I had my doubts because last week Mr. Stanley asked Eli what she thought the problem was after she failed to get the car anywhere near the curb or remotely parallel after more than twelve attempts and she said:

"A. This car does not have a parking-assist feature, and,
B. The spot you are asking me to park in is way too small."

Mr. Stanley said that the parking spot was plenty big enough and demonstrated that by parking the car in it himself, then he hopped out, took out a measuring tape, and calculated how far the front and rear tires were from the curb. He got back in the driver's seat and with a look of satisfaction more appropriate for a somewhat larger accomplishment said, "Exactly three inches." But even still Eli dug her heels in and insisted that she needed a "baggier spot."

Then Alex B. Renner said, "Eli's more of a perpendicular parker than a parallel parker," and I said, "So what? You're more of a senior citizen than a kid," and Benj asked, "What's a baggy spot?" and the class was basically over.

Eli and Mr. Stanley were at a standoff.

I basically wanted to say that there was no spot in the world baggy enough for Eli to park a car in but ReThought that comment and didn't say a thing and then Mr. Stanley got out of the car and Alex B. Renner announced that he got an 800 on the SAT math practice test he just took in the back seat while Eli was *not* parking the car and I said I'm not taking the SATs and he said you have to and I said who says and he said just about everyone. And then I said, "What happens if you sign up but don't show up to take the SATs?" And Benj said, "Nothing. Nobody gives a shit if you show up for the SATs, Joel." Then Eli said, "Of course you're taking the SATs," and I said, "No, I'm not." And she said, "Yes, you are." And Alex B. Renner said, "Shut up, Eli. What are you, his mother?" And Eli said, "Please, Joel." And I said, "Okay, that would be a maybe." And we all got out of the car as the boys' track team ran by like a thundering herd of gazelles.

But when we were by our lockers and I was explaining my plan to teach her how to park, Eli said, “What if I crash into one of your dad’s cars?”

And I said, “It won’t matter.”

“What do you mean it won’t matter?”

“Look.” I held up my phone and showed her a picture of the three cars we would be using.

“Wait. *Those* are your dad’s cars?”

“Well, they’re not exactly *his* cars. . . .”

“What do you mean they’re not exactly *his* cars?”

“It’s just a technicality.”

“What does *that* mean?”

“It means that we can borrow them.”

“Sort of the like the eggs and the asparagus? We *sort of* have permission?”

“Exactly.”

Eli grabbed my phone and scrutinized the pictures.

“And if I dent one it would be hard to notice?”

“Really hard.”

“Which one drives?”

“All of them. I’ll just park two of them with a big-ass baggy space in between and then you and I will get in the third car and practice.”

“What if I can’t learn?”

“Then we’ll just keep trying. Plus, the way I figure it, you can’t learn the Stanley way because you’re afraid you’ll dent one of the cars that you’re parking between and this way you can dent them all you want until you get the hang of it. And, Eli, you’re gonna dent them and it’s gonna be fun.”

"Tomorrow?"

"Tomorrow."

"Okay."

"Okay. After Driver's Ed tomorrow, you go home and have dinner and then I'll pick you up at seven."

Eli said, "Okay. But don't count on having any fun, Higgins," and then she headed to class.

But I knew Eli was dead wrong about that 'cause I was having fun already just watching her walk off.

46

THEN ELI'S GOD

messed with the universe.

Like *really* messed with the universe.

On the same day that the Eli-Can't-Parallel-Park Crash-Car-Combat Operation was scheduled for 7:00 p.m., just as we were all waiting for Mr. Stanley to pull up in the Driver's Ed car, which this time the seniors left in the last place he would ever look—exactly where he had parked it the night before—two cop cars pulled in wicked fast right in front of us. Everyone stopped talking, the officers got out, looked around, and then quickly walked over to us. One of them, the tall one with the mustache, looked right at me and asked, "Are you Joel Higgins?"

Eli and Benj stepped backward in unison and Benj put his hands up kind of halfway and I was thinking, *What the fuck?* and *Maybe they're really here for someone else*, and then I managed to spit out, "Yes," but the way it came out sounded like I wasn't completely sure and then I started looking around as if the real Joel Higgins would pop up out of nowhere and explain that this was all a terrible mistake.

The next thirty seconds flew by really fast as one more car—cop car that is—pulled in and the cops standing next to me looked over their shoulders and nodded to that officer and he stayed in his vehicle and then one of the cops, the tall, mustached one standing next to me, asked if I had any weapons on me. And I hesitated because I was shocked by the question but I finally said, "No," and then he asked, "Do you have a gun at home?" and I pretty much had a heart attack.

Like cardiac arrest.

In the corner of my eye I saw Eli and Benj and now Alex B. Renner huddled together near the wall and then all of us turned to look as Mr. Stanley pulled up in the Driver's Ed car, driving slowly and perfectly as he parallel parked in between the two police cruisers. He secured the vehicle at what appeared to be exactly three inches from the curb and then he stepped out of the car and locked it with the key fob before he finally turned toward us. Mr. Stanley slowly took in the situation as if he could not process what was happening and I could see his left eye going haywire, blinking out *Di-di-dit dah-dah-dah di-di-dit*, as he lifted his hands high over his head like he was being arrested. He called over to me, "Joel, is something wrong here?"

Di-di-dit dah-dah-dah di-di-dit.

Di-di-dit dah-dah-dah di-di-dit.

Di-di-dit dah-dah-dah di-di-dit.

Di-di-dit dah-dah-dah di-di-dit.

And half of those *dit*s and *dah*s were my left eye communicating with Stanley's left eye 'cause now both of us were twitching like there just might be no tomorrow.

I was thinking, *How is it possible that the cops know about the gun unless Rooster got picked up and told them but he doesn't even speak and doesn't even know my last name?* so that didn't seem possible and then when I didn't say anything regarding the gun question because I was trying to process all of this the tall cop asked me again, "Do you have a gun at home, son?"

I didn't move or say a thing. Then the other cop said, "We'd like you to come down to the station. Your parents are already there."

And then it hit me like an eighteen-wheel tractor trailer full of gasoline.

Whatever this was, it was really, really bad.

47

THIS IS WHAT IT SOUNDED LIKE

at the police station:

Where did you get the gun? What were you going to do with it? Do you have any other weapons? Are you angry because your friend Andy died? Do you want to kill anyone? Were you planning on killing yourself? What were you going to do with it? Why did you hide it? Was anyone else involved?

That went on in an interrogation room with three different detectives as Jesus, Mary met with another police officer in another room and Jackson stayed with me and basically said over and over again, "Answer truthfully." And, "Joel, is that your gun?" And, "Should he have a lawyer?" and "Joel, tell the truth." And "Jesus, Joel, is that *really* your gun?" And "Joel, answer truthfully."

Here's what happened:

Jacey found the gun in the garage and brought it to kindergarten.
He kept it in his cubby until show-and-tell at 1:45 p.m.
After gym, but before pickup.
Then he showed-and-telled.

It took a long time for me to get that out of the cops.

This is what Jackson told me:

No one got hurt and Jacey's okay.

No one got hurt and Jacey's okay.

No one got hurt and Jacey's okay.

And this is what I said after Jackson told me what had happened:

It's my gun and I never meant for Jace to find it.

It's my gun and I never meant for Jace to find it.

It's my gun and I never meant for Jace to find it.

This is what I repeated over and over again:

I do not want to kill anyone.

I do not have any other weapons.

I am very angry that Andy died but that doesn't make me want to kill anyone.

I am a good person.

I am not a lone wolf or a terrorist or a psychopath.

I'm so sorry.

I am so sorry.

It's all my fault.

I never thought anyone would find the gun.

I never wanted to hurt anyone.

Please forgive me.

PLEASE LET ME SEE JACEY.

Later, Jace told me that they were all sitting in the sharing circle and then when it was his turn to show-and-tell he ran to the cubbies to get his backpack, which he explained you weren't supposed to take out of the cubby area unless it was circle time and show-and-tell, and he took the gun out and held it up and then he told everyone in his class, "I found a gun stuck in the bricks in my garage where I hide my trucks."

Jacey told me that Jeremy Smuts said, "WOW!" And Courtney Ruben said, "My daddy has five guns." But Mrs. Hanson didn't say anything, "for like a long, long time," and then "she looked scared and stood up really, really slow."

Finally, he told me that Mrs. Hanson said, "JACE, PUT DOWN THE GUN!"

And he told her, "But it's my turn. . . ."

Then he told me that he was wearing the police badge when he took the gun out of his backpack and that he had worn it all day.

This is what I knew: This was on me. *As in completely on me.*

But this is where I made the next mistake in my geometric progression.

I told the truth about everything EXCEPT for one thing.

I never told my parents or the cops where I got the gun.

I didn't want to get Rooster in trouble.

This is what I said instead:

I found the gun on the side of the road. Up on Kennedy Boulevard by the Boys & Girls Club. On the right side of the road behind the speed limit sign if you're heading from town.

That was it.

A big lie.

Studded with enough details to make it sound true.

And it was the worst mistake in the entire universe.

48

BUT THEY BASICALLY BELIEVED ME,

so I got to see Jace.

He was wearing the shiny police badge when he walked into the interrogation room where I was being held.

It was lopsided and pinned to his shirt.

It was fake.

The sergeant who brought Jace to me told me that.

This is what Jace said when he saw me:

"JJJJJOOOOOEEEEELLLLL!"

Then he ran toward me and I hugged him and said that it was all my fault and I was so, so sorry.

Jacey cried and I cried and there was a cop in the room with us and then I said I'm so glad that you're safe and I never wanted to hurt you and you should never touch a gun and why were you in the garage by the bricks and he said, "That's a secret spot where I keep my trucks sometimes." And I said you should know better and I should know better and what were you thinking and Mom is going to kill me and then

Jacey said, "Joel, I got in big trouble for bringing your gun to school," and I said, "I know, buddy."

"I got brought to the principal's office and the police station and Mrs. Hanson said, 'PUT THE GUN DOWN, JACE!!!' And I put the gun down and I didn't shoot anyone not even by accident."

When they took Jace out of the room, Jackson asked the sergeant if I was going to be arrested and if he was sure that I didn't need a lawyer and the cop said, "No, he isn't going to be arrested." And then the cop with the mustache said that at this point, as far as they were concerned, this appeared to be a terrible mistake and that for the time being I wouldn't be charged with anything other than possibly with possession of an unregistered weapon but they were confiscating the gun and would run it through the system to see if it had been fired or had a record and Jace and I would likely be able to go back to school but that was up to the district and it would likely be after a hiatus so they could talk to the other students and the parents who were all outraged and worried. I asked if I could still go to work at the soup kitchen and the cop said, "That's not up to the police. You're a free citizen but don't do anything to hurt anyone." And I said, "Why would I hurt anyone?" And he said, "Because you had a gun." And then Jackson said, "Joel, stop talking." And then one of the detectives said, "Son, you didn't keep the gun away from a tender-aged child." And I wanted to say, *You didn't keep the gun away from a tender-aged child MEANING ME or a mentally ill person MEANING ROOSTER and I didn't know Jacey kept his trucks in the pile of bricks in the garage and I didn't know that he would find the gun and bring it to school.* But I didn't say any of that. I ReThought and saved it as a draft in my head and stopped talking just like Jackson said.

Then everyone said, "Thank God no one got hurt," over and over again and Jesus, Mary came out of a room with a social worker and Jace and a detective, and my mom hugged me and started to cry and shake and I thought, *Thank God I took the bullet out before I put the gun back in the plastic bag the last time I had it out.*

TEXT FROM JOEL TO ANDY 7:47 p.m.

I found one thing I'm really good at.

Lying.

49

WHEN WE GOT HOME

Jacey and I got sent to our rooms but not before we were grilled on illegal activities and weapons possession by Jackson and Jesus, Mary.

I said I had no weapons in my room or the garage or anywhere else. Jacey said he had a pair of sharp scissors—not the blunt-tipped safety kindergarten kind—and Jesus, Mary said, "Hand them over."

Then Jesus, Mary had to go because her cell phone was ringing nonstop. All sorts of people were calling from the two schools and the newspapers and neighbors were saying, "Is there anything we can do?" And she and Jackson had an emergency phone meeting with the superintendent of schools on account of the fact that I might have been planning an attack or been part of a plan to do something horrible. Later Jackson explained that state law mandated a one-year suspension if a student brings a weapon to school but since Jacey was only five and the gun was unloaded and he had no intention of committing an act of violence they had leeway in his case. And then he told us that they would have counselors at both schools all day tomorrow and that me and Jace had to stay home for three days so everyone could calm down and he and my mom would have to go address the parents at a special meeting at Shady Brook on Friday to explain that what happened was not what it looked like. And if that went well then we could go back to school on Monday. If not, Jesus, Mary said, we would have to go to Catholic school. And I was thinking, *Oh no. Not more God.*

Then I overheard my mom telling Jackson that there are two choices: St. Clare of Assisi in White Plains and St. Pat's in Rye. And she added, "If they won't take them, then—"

But Jackson interrupted her, saying, "Jesus, Mary, they would have to take them. It's the church, for Christ's sake."

Either way—Catholic school or regular school—we would both have to go to a therapist because the school insisted that there could be psychological ramifications that needed early intervention, plus it was "mandated protocol in situations like this." I was hoping they assigned someone better than Mrs. Wilson for me, what with how she handled the fight with Mr. Kutchner and my upset-ed-ness over Andy's death last year.

Later that night Jackson stuck his head in my room and said, "Joel, are you okay?" And I said, "I think so." And then he said, "Look, at this point, it is what it is. But this could have ended a very different way."

And we both looked at the floor because we knew what that could have been.

I added, "But you didn't even yell at me or punish me." And Jackson said, "This is way too big for that."

And I knew he was right.

"We'll talk more tomorrow, and we'll fix this," Jackson said, and it was the best thing that my pop ever said to me in my entire life. Then he said that he knew that I would never hurt anyone, especially Jacey, and that I made a terrible mistake bringing a gun into the house and hiding the gun in the garage but that it was fixable and then I cried like I had never cried in my entire life.

Then Pop hugged me and said, "I have to take your phone, Joel. The police asked me to monitor any incoming calls or texts tonight. Nothing official. But just in case."

I handed it over.

And I said, "I am so, so sorry."

And Jackson said, "I know you are. But I want you to remember that being sorry hardly ever fixes anything. And that's worth remembering."

50

TEXT FROM BENJ TO JOEL 11:07 p.m.

Joel, my aunt said you might be a school shooter but I know you R not a bad person.

TEXT FROM JOEL TO BENJ 11:09 p.m.

It's Joel's dad. I took Joel's phone. I will tell him.

TEXT FROM BENJ TO JOEL 11:11 p.m.

Oh. Maybe leave off the part about what my aunt said.

TEXT FROM BENJ TO JOEL 11:12 p.m.

Is Jacey okay?

TEXT FROM JOEL TO BENJ 11:16 p.m.

Yes.

TEXT FROM BENJ TO JOEL 11:23 p.m.

Is Joel okay?

TEXT FROM JOEL TO BENJ 11:30 p.m.

Everyone's okay.

Are you okay, Benj?

TEXT FROM BENJ TO JOEL 11:33 p.m.

I think so.

* * *

TEXT FROM ELI TO JOEL 11:37 p.m.

Are you ok? I'm worried.

TEXT FROM JOEL TO ELI 11:41 P.M.

It's Joel's dad. I have his phone. He's ok.

TEXT FROM ELI TO JOEL 11:42 p.m.

Thank you, Mr. Higgins. I've been praying for all of you.

51

AFTER A FEW DAYS THINGS PRETTY MUCH CALMED DOWN

and everyone forgot about the fact that Jace brought a gun to school and no one really thought I was hoarding weapons or starting a militia or going to show up and shoot up the school anymore.

Jace had to go meet with a therapist two times a week and he could never remember her name, so Jackson started calling her Dr. Crayon on account of the fact that Jacey said all they did was color pictures together. But apparently there was "reason to be concerned" according to Dr. Crayon, who said that when she asked Jacey to draw a picture of his family he always drew Jackson and Jesus, Mary and himself way smaller than me. Dr. Crayon was worried that this was indicative of my "dominance over the family," and Jesus, Mary was reporting all of this to Jackson when they were standing in the kitchen and acting like I wasn't there. As Jackson looked at the pictures Jace had drawn, he said, "Jesus, Mary, that's a bunch of psychobabble bullshit!" Then he yelled, "Hey, Jacey," and Jace ran into the kitchen and Jackson held up one of the drawings of me looking like the Incredible Hulk and them looking like little ants with giant eyes and hands and said, "Hey, Jace, why is Joel so big in this picture?" And Jace took the drawing from him and looked at it carefully and then said, "Because, Jackson, he's my BIG brother and that's how big brothers look! They look BIG."

We all just looked at him and then he said, "Can I go now?"

Jesus, Mary kissed the top of his head and said, "Yes, you can."

Jackson said, "See? Psychobabble bullshit," and then he went to work.

I had to go to therapy with Mrs. Wilson two times a week and the deal was that if she wrote up a good report at the end of the year basically saying that I wasn't messed up and wasn't likely to kill anyone then I wouldn't have to see her next year if I didn't want to. Mrs. Wilson had concerns, though. She asked me if I knew what post-traumatic stress disorder was and when I told her that I did she sat back in her chair and said, "Tell me." And I said, "PTSD is when you've been to a real traumatic place and it hurts your brain, not in a physical way, but a psychological way that makes coming back to normal really hard and it can manifest as panic and anxiety and sometimes as flash-backs and delusions that can be triggered by anything, a loud noise or a memory flash or even a feeling."

Mrs. Wilson looked rightfully impressed and she said, "Nice, Joel."

And then I said, "It's because when you go back to the place that is supposed to be your home after being in an emotional atrocity, sometimes it doesn't feel like home anymore even though you speak the language and you lived there your entire life. You have everything there, your family is there, and maybe you even have a girlfriend who is waiting for you but it's just that when you are traumatized and go away and come back like that, it can seem different, so different, when you return. And not so much because home changed but because you changed.

That place you were, even though it was more awful than you could have imagined and there was horror going on, now it can feel more like home to you in that bad place than it does in your real home. That bad place makes more sense to you now that nothing makes sense plus your buddies were there and you miss them and sometimes when you come home from horror and your girlfriend wants you to look at wedding dresses and she says, 'Which one do you like better? The one with the pearled bodice or the one with the long train?' or she tells you that her friend got a new car or that her boss eats the same sandwich every day you just look at her with a blank stare because she never saved your ass when a bomb was about to go off and everything she is saying sounds like something that you can't understand and you want to tell her that there are places, the places you have been that are covered in sand, so much sand that you can't see clearly or breathe anymore. And when you are there in those bad places you can't shower for weeks and if you sit too long in the same position you can get deep vein thrombosis and a clot can travel to your brain or your lungs and kill you, and you learn on day one that a soldier's creed is *no man left behind* and that you should chamber your last round so you can't be taken alive and the first thing you do if your hand is blown off is apply a tourniquet so you don't bleed out and you are never safe in those places even when you are sleeping and things can just blow up around you with no notice because everyone looks like a civilian but they might be carrying guns or planting improvised explosive devices and there are little kids running around and you can't tell who to save because they all look the same to you because they are just people and you can't tell who is an enemy. And you want to tell your girlfriend this in a language that she can understand because she can't understand so you say to her, 'Imagine that you are at

Target or Kohl's and you are pushing your cart around and trying to decide if you need to buy a garden hose or new sheets or you are wondering if you are out of paper towels and then there is an explosion that is so loud or maybe it's just inside your head but either way now you can't hear anything anymore and yet you feel it reverb in your chest like your ribs are splitting open and then there is a second blast, this one is maybe in the sheet department or maybe it's just inside you and no one else feels it and then there is another explosion in the toy department and then the sporting goods department is on fire and then the whole store is just gone and you are *gone* or maybe just some of you is gone or maybe it looks like you are all there but then the doctors say they don't have the parts they need to make you whole.'

"And then your girlfriend just looks at you and you know that it will never be the same with her because even though you are both speaking English, you are not home. PSTD is like nuclear fallout and radiation and it can do that kind of shit to your head."

Mrs. Wilson sat back in her chair.

I sat back in my chair.

Neither one of us talked for a long time. Then Mrs. Wilson said, "Joel, I think you are going to have to see me in the fall."

I said, "I agree."

And then I said, "Can I go now?"

52

THE NEXT NIGHT, ROOSTER

came into the soup kitchen just like he had been doing every other Wednesday and he stood inside the doorway like he usually did waiting for me to walk toward him so I could go watch his stuff.

I saw that Eli stopped what she was doing and she came over and whispered, "Joel, I see the bear," and I said, "Me too," and then she went to make him a plate of food. Normally people had to get a tray and get in line but Eli always brought Rooster a tray of food herself to entice him, and Mrs. T looked the other way and she never said anything about us breaking the rules or anything. Rooster was wearing Benj's orange socks on his feet and had Benj's blue socks on his hands like they were mittens. I stood by the kitchen door watching and I saw Benj eyeing him with a dumbstruck look on his face like he had just solved a puzzle that had been bugging him for a while as he stood there putting two and two together and getting exactly four. He came over to me and said, "Joel, are those . . ." but he must have ReThought it because after a minute he just walked away without finishing the sentence. Then Rooster took his hat off and I noticed that he had a gash on his forehead that was bleeding and then I saw Mrs. T heading over and she pointed up at his head and Rooster started to get upset. He pulled away from her a bit and started walking backward like he was going to leave and I went over to try to coax him back and then Eli started walking toward him with a tray of food.

I said, "Here you go," taking the tray from Eli and putting it down on a table near the door and then I said, "Why don't you sit here and I'll go watch your stuff?" Rooster looked at the exit and then at the food and then he sat down and I went outside to babysit his cart.

Mrs. T followed me outside and I waved at Rooster, giving him the thumbs-up when I got to his shopping cart. Mrs. T said, "Thanks for that, Joel. You handled it well." She looked like she really meant it and I nodded my head and then she said, "Look. I think that cut of his needs to be looked at. I can call the police and they'll send the paramedics over and they can treat it right here. Assuming he cooperates." She looked at me for a minute and then added, "What do you think?"

I said, "I think it's a really bad idea."

She said, "But that gash looks like it might be infected and it could need stiches."

So I said, "What if we asked him first?"

"I just did."

And I said, "We could try again." Then I added, "Can I do it?"

And she said, "You sure?"

I looked in through the window and Rooster was sitting there by himself eating and I said, "You know what? Let's wait until he comes outside and I'll try to talk to him out here 'cause I don't want to leave his stuff and for whatever reason I think he's more comfortable out here than he is in there."

"Well, just so you know, if we call an ambulance they will likely be here in just a few minutes and they can treat him right out here on the street. They won't take him anywhere he doesn't want to go or arrest him and he doesn't have to pay anything either. They just want to help, not make things worse."

"Are you sure?" I asked as I looked in through the window at Rooster eating, worried that in trying to help we would make things worse for him. Then Mrs. T said, "I've done it a thousand times, Joel, and he can refuse treatment at any point. As far as I know it is not a crime to have a cut on your face. But just so you know, the police will come as well, just in case."

"Okay. I'll ask him when he comes out and if he says yes, I'll wave at you and you can make the call?"

"Sounds like a plan. But don't push too hard and don't get yourself hurt." And when she said it she looked really happy.

Mrs. T went inside and in a few minutes Rooster got up and he returned his tray like he was supposed to and then he came outside and I said, "My name's Joel," which was a weird and awkward thing to say at this late stage in our relationship but I didn't know how else to start a conversation.

Rooster looked at me.

"Does that cut hurt? It looks like it hurts."

He didn't say anything but he raised his hand to his forehead.

"Look," I said. "Mrs. Torrington, the lady who runs this place, she's real nice and I trust her and she said that we could call an ambulance and they could treat that wound for you right here on the sidewalk."

Rooster didn't nod or do anything; he was just ignoring me and moving things around in his shopping cart like everything was now in all the wrong places.

"I could stay with you until they finish. And I'd watch your stuff," I tried.

He didn't look at me or move.

"Should we do that? What do you think?" I asked.

Nothing.

"Hold up one finger if it's a yes. . . ."

Rooster turned back toward me and slowly lifted up one finger.

I saw Mrs. T standing at the window and I gave her a wave and she nodded and Rooster sat down on the curb.

Then I said, "Look, do you want some cake?"

Nothing.

"If you wait here, I can go get it."

Still nothing. Then one finger for yes.

I said, "Hold on. Don't go anywhere," then ran inside and grabbed my backpack and then a piece of cake and a fork from Eli and she said, "Tell him there's more if he wants it."

And I said, "I will."

53

I HAD WINNIE-THE-POOH

in my backpack on account of the fact that Jace and I had the dentist after school and I had promised to read it to him when we were waiting but Dr. Hartman was on time and they took Jace right when we got there and me right after him, so I didn't get to read to Jace at all.

I sat down on the curb next to Rooster and gave him the piece of double-layer Dutch chocolate cake with vanilla icing and red and yellow sprinkles and then I took the book out of my backpack and opened it to the first page and just started reading out loud from the beginning about Christopher Robin and the Hundred Aker Wood, mostly because it was easier than trying to make conversation with someone who didn't talk back. I did it because it would pass the time and also because this book had a calming effect on Jace and me and I thought that maybe it would be distracting to Rooster while we waited. It was only just after six and people were walking and driving by being that the stores were still open and I figured that it must have looked pretty silly for me to be sitting on the curb on Hendricks Street reading a little kid's book to a big old bear of a man with a shopping cart full of junk and too many clothes on who was eating cake, but I didn't care.

Today, in English class, because of the parent complaints about the gay books and the new policy in the school district about violent words, Mr. Morgan listed all of the trigger words and topics in the book we were about to start that might be upsetting to some kids in the class—Iran, hanging people, restrictions on free speech, oppressive governments, revolution, exile, hijabs, the oppression of women, and books about sex. Then he said that anyone who wanted to could leave and go to a safe space next to the principal's office to color.

Nobody left except Paulie Pullman, the same kid who left last time.

Then Mr. Morgan told us about *Reading Lolita in Tehran*, which is a true story about a teacher who read forbidden books with women students in Iran, a country where they have morality police who don't let people read whatever they want to read and where they can't dance, or drink alcohol, or listen to forbidden music except in secret, and women and men can't interact without supervision and if you touch a girl's hand in a park and she isn't related to you you could both be arrested and women can't dress the way they want to and if you are gay you could be put to death and they could display your body on a rope hanging on the back of a truck in the middle of a city to scare other people from doing anything wrong like reading a book or touching a girl's hand in a park or being the way they were born. I was thinking a lot about what Mr. Morgan was saying about free speech being something we should protect even if that meant that sometimes we had to hear stuff that made us uncomfortable and how lucky we were to be able to read whatever we wanted to read whenever we wanted to read it even if that only meant sitting on the curb and reading a book out loud to a man who has a Purple Heart that came with delusions and a heartbreak of an illness that nobody could fix.

When the cop car pulled up I was at the part where Christopher Robin is explaining to Pooh that you don't get honey with balloons. The cops came over and Mrs. T came out to talk to them. Then the Colonel and Spindini came outside and sat down next to us on the curb. I was reading the part where Pooh Goes Visiting and Gets Into a Tight Place when the ambulance pulled up with its lights on but no siren. The paramedics were really cool and they asked Rooster's permission to look at the cut on his face and I kept reading as they cleaned up the wound and they kept asking Rooster if they could do this or do that without me even pausing to let them talk. I was at the part where Pooh gets stuck in Rabbit's hole when Eli came outside and I kept reading as one of the paramedics told Rooster that the cut didn't need stitches, so they were going to put a big butterfly bandage across it and they told him that they used antibiotic cream so it would heal better and I was at the part where all Rabbit's friends and relations went head-over-heels backward to pull Pooh free from the entrance to Rabbit's house and Eli was sitting on the curb next to Spindini at this point and when the paramedics were done, one of them, a big guy with a shaved head, told Rooster he did two tours of duty in the "sandbox," which he said, for those of us who didn't know, was Iraq. He said he was a Navy hospital corpsman, which is a medic in the Marines. Then he said he never read *Winnie-the-Pooh* and one of the cops said, "Are you fucking kidding me, man?" And then the cop said his favorite part was near the end when Piglet Does a Very Grand Thing and I said that my favorite part was the beginning because it's as far as it can be from being over. And then he asked Rooster if he could do anything for him like give him a ride to a shelter and I was wondering why things like this weren't in the police blotter. I mean, come on.

Rooster didn't say anything, he just got up and took his cart, and all of us, me and Eli, and the cops and the paramedics, and Spindini and the Colonel, and Mrs. T just stood there watching as he walked away with the butterfly bandage and antibacterial cream and us figuring that we all did what we could even though we were all wishing like hell that we could have done more. Maybe even a Very Grand Thing, like heroically pulling someone who was stuck out of a very tight place.

TEXT FROM JOEL TO PRINCIPAL REDMAN 4:09 a.m.

Here's a sentence completion for the SAT people.

If a town in Rockland County has a large number of people who are --------- who don't have enough ---------, the town should just ---------.

A. veterans, food, do the bare minimum

B. criminals, places to rob, leave all the bank doors unlocked

C. religious, churches, suggest they become atheists

D. skateboarders, skateboard parks, build more

The correct answer is "D." The skateboard one.

"A" is tricky. I mean, the SAT people would mark it wrong, but it's pretty much what happens.

54

THE NEXT DAY AT SCHOOL BENJ SAID,

"Did you Google Burning Man?"

I said, "How is your penny project?"

He said that he ran into a stumbling block.

And I said, "Day fifteen?"

And he said, "How did you know?"

Then I said, "Burning Man sounds cool, but I still can't go."

And Benj said, "Did you ask Jackson?"

"No."

"Jesus, Mary?"

"No."

"Just wait. You'll change your mind." Then Benj said, "Here," and handed me a plastic bag full of socks in a variety of colors and a pair of winter gloves.

Men's size large.

And then he just walked away.

55

THE NEXT WEEK A KID CAME INTO THE SOUP KITCHEN

who looked like he was our age, and I watched as Mrs. T went over to talk to him.

I was wiping down tables with a rag and Eli was somewhere in the back and when the kid got in line to get food Mrs. T waved at me to follow her. When we reached the kitchen she waved Eli and Benj over and told us that the boy's name was Jesse and that it might be nice if we tried to talk to him. "He just told me that he grew up in foster care moving from home to home, but when he turned eighteen he aged out of the system. The state wouldn't give anyone money to keep him, so that's it." And then Mrs. T started piling dishes into the sink like she was trying to break all of them and then she added, "Jesse probably doesn't have most of the basic life skills he needs to take care of himself. He didn't even get to graduate from high school."

She pretty much said that he was in a hole and didn't have a ladder to climb out.

I said, "There has to be a way," and Mrs. T basically told us that there wasn't and that it sucked but at least we are here to give him a hot meal.

Me and Eli and Benj went back out front and sat down with Jesse. We were wearing T-shirts that said *Hendricks Street Soup Kitchen* on the front and Jesse looked at them and then down at his food and I said, "Hey, my name's Joel and this is Benj and Eli," and he said, "I don't want to be your research subject or pity project."

I said, "It's not like that."

And Jesse looked at the three of us again and said, "Yes, it is."

Then Eli said, "Do you want some cake?" And Jesse said, "Yes, please," and Eli got up to get Jesse a piece of cake and when she came back we all sat there while he ate it with his gloves on and we didn't say anything but we all stared out the window as a girl was getting into her car with her mother and she was laughing and talking to someone on her cell phone and they had huge white bags from Bed Bath & Beyond that were full of what looked like stuff for a new apartment or to bring to college 'cause there were big pillows and velvet hangers and a coffeepot and a Swiffer handle was sticking out of one of the bags. There were so many bags that they had trouble fitting them all in the car. I was thinking about what Mr. Morgan told us about high schools and colleges where there are safe spaces to protect students from the violence of words and I was thinking that there were no safe spaces to protect kids like Jesse from the violence of life if they don't have a family. And then I was thinking that Jesse must feel really bad because that girl has a safe space from the violence of life with velvet hangers and big soft pillows and he doesn't, and even if he did have velvet hangers and big soft pillows he wouldn't have a closet to hang them in or a bed to put them on and that sure felt like a fucking hole that would be impossible to climb out of.

I looked over at Benj and was wondering what he was thinking at this point and then I looked at Eli and wanted to say, "Where's your God now?" but ReThought and didn't say anything at all.

I just shut up and sat there.

Jesse never came back after that night.

At least not on a Wednesday.

56

MRS. T TOLD US

that we had to write an essay or do a piece of artwork or anything else creative about our experience working in the soup kitchen to hand in to Mr. Morgan as part of our community service requirement.

She said it didn't have to be a big project but it had to be from the heart.

Benj painted a picture of Spindini eating.

In the picture Spindini had a giant head and a giant fork and giant hands and pretty much it didn't look like Spindini or even a man eating but it was more like modern art where you had to bring your imagination, or if you didn't have an imagination then you just had to listen to what the artist said it was a picture of and take his word for it. Eli said it reminded her of a Picasso and Mrs. T said it was more like a Basquiat and I said I didn't know who they were but it looked exactly like a Jacey Higgins to me.

I submitted a pair of socks.

Quite possibly the last pair in the Higgins house.

And Eli made a birthday card.

On the front was a picture of me as a homeless person in ripped, dirty clothes wearing a backpack. She Photoshopped my face onto an image of a guy in crappy clothes but Benj said, "I don't get it. That's what Joel looks like every day."

I said, "Is not."

Benj said, "Is too."

Eli said, "Cut it out."

On the front of the card it said, *Happy Birthday!*

Inside it said, *This is what I would give you if I could:*

1. *A house with doors and windows and a roof*
2. *A job*
3. *A plan*
4. *Enough food so you were never hungry*
5. *Books*
6. *Love*
7. *Shoes*
8. *Clothes*
9. *Socks*
10. *A wallet full of cash*
11. *A healthy brain*
12. *Toothpaste*
13. *A healthy body*
14. *Free medicine*
15. *A TV*
16. *A cell phone with unlimited data*
17. *A car*
18. *A coffeepot*

19. A different world
20. A friend
21. A lot of friends
22. A safe space
23. God
24. A promise that I will try to make things better

Benj said real birthday cards usually weren't that big and what Eli wrote would never fit on one and Eli said it was her magnum opus and Benj said what is that and she said my masterpiece and I said we would make it fit, Benj.

He said no you wouldn't.

I said we'd have to. Those are violent words.

TEXT FROM JOEL TO ANDY 1:54 a.m.

Jackson and me played crash-car combat and annihilated a BMW 380i and a Subaru Outback last weekend. They were pretty busted up when we got them but you should have seen it.

The Subaru won. I was driving it. Jackson was pissed. I mean, come on, he had the Beamer.

TEXT FROM JOEL TO PRINCIPAL REDMAN 3:52 a.m.

Here are some more words that should NOT be on the SAT:

Napiform—resembling a turnip
Mundungus—malodorous tobacco or half blood wizard in Harry Potter
Ort—a scrap of food left after eating
Oxter—armpit

And here is a possible sentence completion you might suggest to the SAT people because this one actually makes sense:

The conclusion of his argument, while _______, is far from_______.

Is it:

A. stimulating - interesting
B. abstruse - incomprehensible
C. germane - relevant
D. worthwhile - valueless
E. esoteric - obscure
F. out there - total bullshit

The answer's "F."
The SAT people will tell you "B" works too,
but basically the answer is "F."

TEXT FROM JOEL TO ANDY 4:06 a.m.

The exploding head syndrome calmed down, so I might not have a brain tumor but now I have a nasty rash to go along with the fungus. And Jackson's still a mess. But don't worry.

57

ON OUR LAST DAY IN THE SOUP KITCHEN

Hendricks Street Will Smith came back and he was wearing a business suit.

He said he would like the chicken, no salad, please and he said his name was Sam Trenton and he used to be a software engineer for a tech company but he got into some financial trouble and then he couldn't get a job when the recession hit in 2008 and he lost his house and then he got sick and didn't have health insurance and his wife left him and divorce is really expensive and the tech bubble burst and companies don't hire old people like him especially in tech where being over forty is like being a hundred. And then he said Margot Kidder was homeless once and and lived in a cardboard box in California and she was Lois Lane in *Superman*. Then he said Sugar Ray Williams, who was captain of the Knicks and played for the Boston Celtics, had to sleep in his car when he became homeless because he made some bad investments and spent too much money. Then Sam Trenton said, "Shit like that happens all the time."

I said, "Did you see the Will Smith movie where Will Smith is homeless and has a kid played by his real son in real life and he wears a business suit and is trying to get back on his feet and they sleep in the bathroom in the subway and he ends up getting a good job?"

Hendricks Street Will Smith nodded his head yes and said, "Come on, man, that wasn't believable because it was freakin' Will Smith for Christ's sake."

I said, "I know, right?"

And then Hendricks Street Will Smith said, "I cried at that movie," and I said, "I know. Me too."

58

THEN IN THE SECOND-TO-LAST WEEK OF DRIVER'S ED,

Mr. Stanley announced that he had a surprise for us.

Now, there were rampant rumors going around school as to exactly what Mr. Stanley's surprise was—after all, this wasn't the first time that he had taught Driver's Ed. If you listened to the seniors they'd tell you that he'd been here at CC High since the Ford Motor Company rolled out the first assembly line vehicle in 1913 but Alex B. Renner said, "They didn't have Driver's Ed back then and Calf City High didn't open until 1952." Plus, Stanley told us on the first day of class that he started teaching at CC in 1971, so I mean, come on, do the math. Eddie Casonov said Mr. Stanley's surprise was that he took you to the King Kone stand up on Route 127 and bought everyone in the car an ice cream. The kind of soft-serve ice-cream cone that is dipped in a hot chocolate glaze that turns solid but it makes the ice cream inside so soft that it drips down onto your hands when you try to eat it. I knew that 'cause when we stopped at King Kone with Jace when Jesus, Mary wasn't with us, Jackson would tell him he had two choices—a dish or a cone. But the cone came with a trip through the car wash. Jace would get a real serious look on his face and he always said, "They don't let kids go through the car wash, Jackson," and get this, he added, "*For out a car*." And I would say, "Jace, you mean *without a car*," and he would say, "That's what I said, Joel!" Jace was either way braver and way tougher than me, or else he thought the cone was worth it because he always picked the cone and the car wash, not the dish. Made a bigger mess than you'd think was possible, too. From his hair to his sneakers needed to be hosed down as he was covered in chocolate and Jace always looked a little scared anyway—not *really scared*, but just a little—his eyes dartin' to me, then back to the car wash as we drove by it.

Other seniors just smiled and said, "Ice-cream cone? No fuckin' way, man. But you'll see." And I'd heard some weird rumors, too. Some kids said that Mr. Stanley took you out onto Route 287 on a long, straight strip of highway between exits 65 and 66 and then he took his foot away from the special brake pedal they install for the Driver's Ed teacher and he made the kid driving step on the gas till the pedal hit the floor and the speedometer flirted with a hundred miles per hour as the little compact car started rattling to the bone 'cause the tin can piece of shit Ford Fiesta wasn't stable at that speed. The seniors said he did it to teach us a lesson about drag racing and speeding. I didn't know what was true and what was just shit kids made up to scare each other, but me? Personally? I didn't care much for an ice-cream cone 'cause I'd have way rather seen Mr. Stanley yell, "Floor it, bitch!" as Alex B. Renner gripped the wheel and flew down the highway in the passing lane while me and Benj and Eli hung on tight in the back seat wondering if we were gonna die as Mr. Stanley was wringing his hands and his eye was twitching some message . . . *dah-di-dit dah-dah-dah dah-dit-dah* . . . as the world went by the car windows way faster than we would ever see it do again in our lifetimes with old Mr. Stanley's lid dancing *dit*s and *dah*s in rhythmic patterns galloping like a horse to water . . . *dah-di-dit di-dah-dit di-dit dah-dit dah-di-dah* . . . as the grassy hills of Rockland County flew by the economy car's windows at warp speed with Benj playing What if, saying, "Joel, what if you modified the Driver's Ed car and turned it into a time machine powered by plutonium stolen from Libyan terrorists just like in the movie *Back to the Future* and you drove so fast that we broke through the time/space barrier and then we went back in time and fixed things?"

And I'd ask, "Fixed what, Benj?"

And he'd say, "Fucking everything."

And I would say, "Hell yes, let's do it!"

Then I would blast right through any fucking barriers there were and we would fix all of it. Benj's dead parents, Jace and the gun, Rooster, Andy's cancer, PTSD, Spindini, the Colonel, Jesse, Hendricks Street Will Smith . . .

But that's not what happened.

There was no crazy "Mr. Stanley's lost it" moment. No Alex B. Renner behind the wheel of the Ford Fiesta as Mr. Stanley yelled, "Floor it, bitch!" and no Joel Higgins behind the wheel breaking through the time/space barrier.

And no ice cream either.

Nothing like that.

Not even close.

Mr. Stanley's surprise was waiting for us right up on the winding backcountry roads of the hill section of town, not on Route 287 or any other highway.

When we were driving that day, Mr. Stanley told Alex B. Renner to pull to the side of the road, right at the same spot where the path to the Richardsons' farm was. Right near the path where me and Eli cut in to collect eggs and asparagus and where I'd seen Rooster pushing his cart that first day. Then Stanley had him turn the engine off and he told us all to get out of the car. Mr. Stanley had us walk a few yards in from the side of the road as his eye was going haywire . . . *di-dah dah-dit dah-di-dit* . . . and then he told the four of us standing in the tall grass that this exact spot was where Abby Louise died.

Kutchner leaned in to me and whispered, "Who the hell is Abby Louise?"

And Mr. Stanley told us.

"Twenty-seven years ago, Abby Louise came around that curve in the road." Mr. Stanley was pointing up to a spot right before the Richardsons' farm where the road bent at ninety degrees. "And she swerved into this tree." We were standing in front of a big oak that'd been there a hundred years or more.

"Dead on impact. Skull smashed in."

Eli let out a whimper.

"Drunk driving accident. Blood alcohol level of point two-oh." Stanley's eye twitching away . . . *dah-di-dit di-dah-dit di-dit di-di-di-dah-dit*. "I just wanted you to know that."

Then while we all stood there looking at the tree and imagined hitting it at high speed and taking in the sum total of what Mr. Stanley had said, he added, "Abby Louise was my daughter. She was four days short of her seventeenth birthday."

Eli was whimpering and looking at her feet and Mr. Stanley's eye was going *di-di-dit dah-dah-dah di-di-dit* twitching out a message nobody could understand and Eli converted that whimper to a full-blown cry and Alex B. Renner was just looking at the ground and kicking at the dirt and grass and I was thinking that I had been a total ass for not being nice to Mr. Stanley and I could add that to the everything-that-is-wrong-with-Joel column of one of Eli's lists and then I was thinking about telling him I was sorry and then I was thinking about putting my arm around Eli, but Benj did it first. He draped his arm around her and she tucked right into his chest and started to sob. Then Mr. Stanley said, "Come on now, all of you get back in the car. I'll drive." Mr. Stanley got in the front seat driver's side and Alex B. Renner hopped into the back seat and me and Eli were in line to climb into the back after him, which left Benj in position to ride shotgun, when Eli saw something out of the corner of her eye and she suddenly turned and was now standing just a foot in front of me with her face drawn and wet and pale from all that crying. Her eyes were just about drilling a hole through the front of my head and even though it was completely inappropriate under the circumstances I was thinking about kissing her right there in front of everyone, when she grabbed hold of my shoulders and very serious like as if she had seen a ghost said, "Joel, I see the bear."

And my heart went cold.

Ice-cold.

'Cause I knew that Rooster was standing right behind me.

AND I KNEW THAT EITHER

I had to make a move immediately, or something bad was going to happen.

That much was written all over Eli's face.

And then it happened.

And Joel Higgins wasn't fast enough or strong enough for the likes of the man we called Rooster.

I heard a loud explosion and a piercing scream and a thud and a door slam and a male voice moan in anguish and then a commotion and then I heard feet sliding, then a dragging noise and then another scream that might have come from Benj or Eli—I wasn't sure which—then a whimper and that sickening scream again and someone said, "Oh shit!" and I turned around and saw Rooster standing ten yards back directly behind me.

And he was holding a gun.

I turned slightly to my left in what felt like slow motion and I saw Benj Kutchner on the ground in a puddle of blood.

There was so much blood.

And I was trying real hard to connect the dots and nothing at all made sense and then I saw Eli fall to her knees and then she was leaning over Benj and covered in blood herself and then I saw Mr. Stanley planted in the roadbed like a statue unmoving but twitching *di-dit dah-dah-dah di-di-dit* and Alex B. Renner was nowhere to be seen but was presumably down on the floor of the back seat of the Ford Fiesta fearing for his life, and I finally unglued my feet from their stationary position and did something to propel myself to action 'cause once again both my feet and brain were rooted in something that kept them from moving for more seconds than I would have liked but then finally, finally, I lunged at Rooster.

I tackled him, wrestled him to the ground, and got hold of the gun and tossed it to the side of the road. Not because I was fierce and strong, but because he wasn't trying to stop me.

Kneeling on top of Rooster with my knees pressing into his chest right there in the road where Mr. Stanley's daughter plowed into a tree and cracked open her skull I looked back over my shoulder and saw Benj still lying on the ground and Eli was still next to him now with both hands pressing hard on his shoulder as she yelled, "Somebody call an ambulance!" And I was trying to put two and two together but was getting nowhere even close to four until I finally figured out the what but not the why.

Rooster had shot Benj Kutchner.

I yelled to Eli, "How bad is he hurt?"

And she yelled back, "I don't know! He's bleeding a lot!"

In that moment Mrs. T's voice resonated in my head—*"We can feed 'em but we can't fix 'em"*—and I screamed, "What the fuck did you go and do that for?" to the big old bear of a man who never spoke.

Then, with one hand around his throat and the gun lying off to the side of the roadway where I had tossed it, I reached into my pants pocket for my cell phone and called 911. I told the operator to send an ambulance to Mill Lane up near the Richardsons' farm. Said that there was a man with a gun who shot a kid. Then I did a double take and looked at that gun, stunned for a moment.

It had never occurred to me that Rooster could have had more than one gun.

Then I heard Spindini's voice telling me that he had a whole collection of guns and then my voice telling the detectives and Jackson and my mom that I found the gun on the side of the road up on King Street near the Boys & Girls Club now knowing that if I had told the truth I could have stopped this and that this, just like the near tragedy with Jace, was on me.

Then, as I knelt there with my knees still pinned against this man's Purple-Hearted chest, I heard my pop's refrain playing in my head. *"It is what it is."* A horrible summation of the fact that shit happens like Mr. Stanley's dead daughter and Benj Kutchner getting shot and his parents getting killed and Jace bringing a gun to school and the vets committing suicide and Andy getting cancer and Rooster suffering from what he was suffering from and my own long string of stupid decisions and that all of it could be so goddamned unfixable just like a blown-out tire or a seized-up transmission and there was nothing anyone could do about any of it no matter how hard we might try. But then, as these last few months were flashing before my eyes with me seething in anger and looking to lay blame and with Eli whimpering over Benj as he lay bleeding in the street and Mr. Stanley still planted in the roadway lightning-struck with terror and Alex B. Renner hiding on the floor of the back seat of the Ford Fiesta, Rooster spoke for the first time since I had met him.

He yelled, "Get back in the fucking Humvee, Joel. That's an order!"

Tears started falling from my eyes and my heart broke in that moment just like a bullet had pierced glass and shattered it into 10.7 million pieces.

And then he yelled again, "We need air support. Get back in the Humvee! Call in air support!"

The sirens were getting closer and closer and I bent down and hugged Rooster. Even though everything was wrong and everything was messed up and it made no sense to hug him. I did it anyway.

He was trying to protect *me*.

It was PTSD and friendly fire.

Then I released myself from the hug and I looked right at him and said, "Hold up one finger if you want me to try to get you help."

Rooster made eye contact with me and I saw it there again in his eyes, that fear, raw and bleeding and too big for any man to conquer alone. But then something clicked in those eyes of his and he slowly lifted his right hand and held up one finger and I hugged him again.

I hugged that big bear of a man even though he did the wrong thing because it seemed like the right thing and because he recognized that he needed help. I hugged him 'cause he fought for this country and came home and nothing made sense anymore and he found out that he had lost himself over there and because when he got home he had parts missing even though they were all there.

I was still five foot eight and Eli was still five foot ten and Abby

Louise Stanley was still dead and Andy was still dead and Jace still brought a gun to school and Rooster still had a Purple Heart that screwed up his head and now Benj Kutchner was shot and bleeding and there was nothing that any one of us could do to change any bit of that.

Not a goddamned-fucking thing.

But right there on that street waiting for that ambulance to pull up and praying real hard that Benj would survive this, I decided that I was sure as hell going to try anyway.

To fix everything going forward.

As best as I could.

60

AND I WAS GOING TO START BY TAKING BENJ

to Burning Man.

My version of it anyway.

Benj had been hit in the shoulder, which the doctors said can be deadly within minutes, but luckily the bullet missed his major arteries and he was going to fully recover. But because of the trauma, everyone was worried about all of us and I was worried about all of us, so a few days after Benj got out of the hospital I texted him to meet me out in front of his aunt's house and I texted Eli to meet me in front of her house and I said that we had to meet up to do something important and they both texted *Okay*, and then I told Jackson that I had to take his truck somewhere for a few hours and he said, "Joel, you don't have your license." And I said, "That's only a technicality." And he said, "Promise you won't do anything stupid or drink and drive or—"

And I said, "Look at this." And I handed him my phone and showed him a text that Eli sent me a few days back:

Every single day 28 people in America die in a drunk-driving accident.
That's 28 Abby Louise Stanleys EVERY SINGLE DAY.

That's 196 Abby Louise Stanleys EVERY SINGLE WEEK.

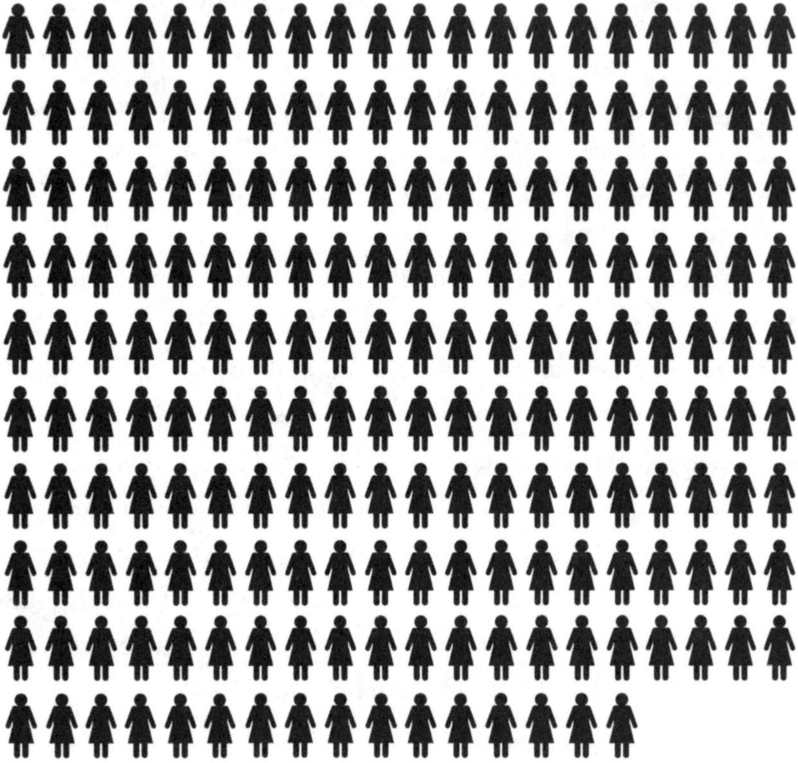

That's 10,220 Abby Louise Stanleys EVERY SINGLE YEAR.
And 10,220 heartbroken Mr. Stanleys EVERY SINGLE YEAR.
And 10,220 heartbroken Mrs. Stanleys EVERY SINGLE YEAR.

Here's the thing.
I don't have enough room for that many Stanleys.
Don't ever drink and drive.

Jackson said, "Eli sent you this?"

"Yep."

"Who is Abby Louise Stanley?"

"My Driver's Ed teacher's daughter."

Jackson said, "Here are the keys. Do what you have to do."

I picked up Benj and his shoulder was bandaged and his arm was in a sling and he said, "Don't look at me like that, Joel. The doctors say I'm going to be back to normal in a few months."

I just nodded my head and then texted Eli again and told her to come out when she saw my dad's truck pull up in front of her house.

I had brought along a can of gasoline, wire cutters, and a lighter. And a sledgehammer and a fire extinguisher.

I was going to make this right.

Or as right as it could be with Benj with a bullet wound in the shoulder and Rooster in the VA hospital.

61

I PARKED

the truck by the tree where Abby Louise died and Benj got shot.

The exact spot that marked the entrance to the path to the Richardsons' farm and Rooster's shanty.

When I pulled in, Eli said, "Joel, this is where Benj was shot. I don't think . . ."

But I ignored her and climbed out of the truck and they followed after me. I grabbed the gas can, the sledgehammer, the wire cutters, and the fire extinguisher from the back, asked both of them to carry something and said, "Come with me."

Eli said, "Joel, you're scaring me."

But I didn't respond.

As we headed down the path Eli asked, "Why are we going to the farm where we came to collect the eggs and pick asparagus?"

I still didn't respond.

"What are you going to do with gasoline?" she asked.

As we headed farther into the woods I said, "Don't worry. Nothing bad." And I took Benj and Eli to Rooster's shanty.

Benj stopped, put the stuff he was carrying down and looked around, and then said, "What is this place?"

But I didn't answer. I just put the gas can and the fire extinguisher down and picked up the sledgehammer.

"Stand back."

"Joel, don't!" Eli looked scared. Real scared.

I started swinging.

"What is this place?" Benj asked again.

"This is Iraq," I said.

I swung again. Hit the walls, the shopping carts, all the shit inside.

"This is Afghanistan."

I swung again and again with each declaration.

"This is mental illness."

The doorway collapsed.

"This is homelessness.

"Hunger.

"Veteran suicide . . ."

The sidewall fell.

"This is dead parents.

"Cancer.

"And dead friends . . ."

The back wall hit the ground. . . .

"This is post-traumatic stress disorder.

"This is Jesse.

"And Spindini . . ."

There was nothing left standing, but I kept swinging.

"And this is wrong.

"This is war . . ."

I stopped. Took it all in. Caught my breath.

"And it's enough."

I put the sledgehammer down and stepped back and Eli asked, "Joel, was Rooster living here?"

I nodded my head.

Benj asked, "Who's Rooster?"

Eli said, "The guy from the soup kitchen who shot you." She wiped away a tear.

Benj looked around, shook his head in disbelief, and then said, "I didn't know he had a name. . . ."

I started to say, "The guys at Hendricks Street who didn't talk . . ." but Eli looked at me and then finished my sentence.

"Sometimes we gave them names."

62

BENJ JUST KEPT NODDING HIS HEAD SLOWLY

as he looked around at all the debris.

Then I took the largest boards I could find and laid them out on the ground and assembled them into the shape of a ten-foot-tall man. I attached the boards together with the old rusty wire and bits of rope that Rooster had used to try to hold his whole life together. First, I fashioned a torso with arms and legs and a head. Next, I started wiring shit to it. Tons of shit. Rooster's newspapers and trash, old paperback books, flyers from grocery stores, empty soda cans, filthy clothes, pairs of my socks.

Lots and lots of my socks.

Jackson's socks.

Benj's bright orange socks became Rooster's feet. Benj's blue socks were Rooster's hands in mittens.

Benj came over and tried to help.

"You're making The Man from Burning Man for me," Benj said, and I nodded my head in agreement.

Everything we strapped to The Man was important. Every empty soup can and pair of socks. It all stood for something. Then Eli jumped in and started picking stuff up and handing it to me.

A tin pie plate, a filthy shirt, a milk carton, a magazine . . .

Then in my frantic scrounging and rampage I picked up one of the medical reports I had seen a few days before:

January 14, 2015 3:10 p.m.
Veteran's Administration Hospital

Patient Notes
Patrick Allen Samson

Rank Master Sergeant/US Marine Corps
Honorable Discharge 2014

IDENTIFYING DATA: PTSD, depression, psychosis, traumatic brain injury.

HISTORY OF PRESENT ILLNESS: The patient is a 33-year-old white male who did two tours of duty in Iraq and one in Afghanistan. He currently lives with his wife and infant daughter. He presented today with extreme agitation and erratic behavior.

PAST MEDICAL HISTORY: PTSD, depression, and substance abuse.

PAST SURGICAL HISTORY: 17 surgeries for cranial reconstruction, shrapnel removal, and hand reconstruction. Amputation at the distal phalange of the index and long finger from left hand.

ALLERGIES: None known.

MEDICATIONS: Sertraline (Zoloft) 200 mg daily. Past use of Venlafaxine (Effexor) 75 mg to 300 mg daily.

REVIEW OF SYSTEMS: Unable to obtain secondary to the patient being in restraints and sedated.

OBJECTIVE: Vital signs revealed a blood pressure of 130/80, pulse of 115, respirations of 22, and temperature is 96.6 degrees Fahrenheit. HEENT, and history and physical examination were unable to be obtained.

LABORATORY DATA: Laboratory reveals slightly elevated glucose at 100.2. Previous urine tox was positive for THC. Urinalysis was negative, CBC normal.

ASSESSMENT AND PLAN:

AXIS I: Psychosis. Inpatient Psychiatric Team to follow.

AXIS II: PTSD.

AXIS III: Deferred.

Evaluation to be followed up by medication adjustment and evidenced-based therapies: CPT and PE.

I read it out loud to Eli and Benj.

Then Eli bent over, picked up another piece of paper and said, "Joel, here's another one. It's from a year later on Christmas Eve."

She read it out loud to us.

December 24, 2015 11:12 a.m.
Veteran's Administration Hospital

Patient Notes
Patrick Allen Samson

Rank Master Sergeant/US Marine Corps
Honorable Discharge 2014

IDENTIFYING DATA: PTSD, depression, psychosis, traumatic brain injury. Apraxia.

HISTORY OF PRESENT ILLNESS: The patient is a 34-year-old white male who did two tours of duty in Iraq and one in Afghanistan. He is currently homeless. He presented today with extreme agitation and erratic behavior and verbally unresponsive. Friend who brought him in said he hasn't spoken in months.

PAST MEDICAL HISTORY: PTSD, depression, and substance abuse.

PAST SURGICAL HISTORY: 17 surgeries for cranial reconstruction, shrapnel removal, and hand reconstruction. Amputation at the distal phalange of the index and long finger from left hand.

ALLERGIES: None known.

MEDICATIONS: Sertraline (Zoloft) 200 mg daily. Past use of Venlafaxine (Effexor) 75 mg to 300 mg daily.

REVIEW OF SYSTEMS: Unable to obtain secondary to the patient being in restraints and sedated.

OBJECTIVE: Vital signs revealed a blood pressure of 140/90, pulse of 110, respirations of 20, and temperature is 96.0 degrecs Fahrenheit. HEENT, and history and physical examination were unable to be obtained.

LABORATORY DATA: Laboratory reveals slightly elevated glucose at 114.2. Previous urine tox was positive for THC. Urinalysis was negative, CBC normal.

ASSESSMENT AND PLAN:

AXIS I: Psychosis. Inpatient Psychiatric Team to follow.

AXIS II: PTSD.

AXIS III: Deferred.

Evaluation to be followed up by medication adjustment and evidenced-based therapies: CPT and PE. Consult on apraxia.

The medical reports were littered all over the place. Piled on the ground. Assembled in folders.

I collected all of them and put them aside and then used them to fashion hair, Medusa-like hair.

I stepped back.

It was done.

Patrick Allen Samson

Rooster had a real name.

THEN I PROPPED THE MAN

right next to the old oak tree where Patrick Allen Samson had pinned me that day when he gave me the plastic bag with the gun in it and I stood back and then me and Benj and Eli just looked at it for a long time.

"What are we going to do now?" Eli finally asked.

And Benj said, "We're gonna burn it."

"Burn it? Why are you doing this, Joel?"

Then Benj said, "I told Joel that I wanted to go to Burning Man so he's doing this for me. That night when I was drunk and Joel picked me up with his dad, I told him that my parents died in a car crash with an eighteen-wheel tractor trailer."

Eli hugged Benj and they both started to cry.

I said, "Benj told me late that night that he never got to say goodbye to them." And then I added, "He told me that at Burning Man they build a beautiful temple where people come from all over the world to leave prayers for the people they have lost."

Eli squeezed both of our hands.

Then Benj said, "Then, after everyone has left their prayers and said goodbye, they burn the temple to the ground with all the prayers inside and they watch the smoke as it rises toward the sky.

"People say that after that experience they feel like they can go on. And they feel closer to God. Not that it takes the loss away, just that they can accept it more."

Then Eli said, "But this is Rooster's stuff, Joel."

And I said, "He told me to do it. I asked him when I went to see him at the hospital a few days ago if he wanted me to get rid of this place and he nodded his head. I asked him if he was sure and he lifted one finger—that's his way of saying yes. I think he knows this isn't right. So I came here yesterday to go through his stuff and I pulled out some things to save for him. Here, look."

I reached into my pocket and pulled out a medal in a little case.

Patrick Allen Samson's Purple Heart.

"I'm going to bring it to him at the hospital."

Eli took it from me, looked at it closely, and then said, "Let's say a prayer."

And I handed them both a pen and said, "How about we say a whole bunch of prayers?"

So that's what me and Benj and Eli did. We wrote prayers on Patrick Allen Samson's medical reports and attached them to The Man with anything we could find—wire, string, nails. . . .

Then I doused The Man in gasoline and lit it on fire.

And Eli and Benj and I stepped way back and watched as it burned.

We watched as the smoke rose toward the heavens and we said goodbye to Benj's parents. To Andy. And to Rooster.

And to a perfect world.

And it felt like the end of everything.

64

AFTER THE FLAMES DIED DOWN A BIT

Eli said that she had to walk back to the truck to get her phone to call her mom.

Once she was gone Benj said, "You know, Joel, even though my parents died and Andy died and Mr. Stanley's daughter's dead and Jacey brought a gun to school and I got shot and there are homeless vets and Eli can't park a car for shit and will never go out with you, we are transitioning from sequential worsening to positive compounding."

This is what I said: "What the fuck are you talking about?"

"The good things are progressing geometrically, too, Joel."

I just looked at him.

"What good things?"

"I'm not dead. Jace didn't shoot the gun. Patrick Allen Samson is going to get help. We're friends now. There's good stuff, too." I kicked at some of the embers and looked back to where Rooster's shanty had been. Then Benj said, "Hey, you didn't object when I said we were friends, so I guess we're officially friends now. Right, Joel?"

I said, "That's a definite maybe, Benj," and smiled.

And Benj said, "Thanks, Joel."

Then Eli came back and I took out my phone.

"Who are you calling?" Eli asked.

"I'm not calling anyone. I'm texting Andy."

Eli's face softened and she put her hand on my arm.

"Andy Westfield?" she asked.

"Yep."

"Joel, Andy's dead," Eli said, like she thought I didn't remember.

"Just because he died it doesn't mean that I can't talk to him, Eli."

Benj said, "He's right, Eli. It's not that weird. I talk to my parents all the time—in the beginning I even left them voice messages—and they're dead, too."

TEXT FROM JOEL TO ANDY 4:43 p.m.

If you start with a penny, and you double it every day, in one month you'd have $10.7 million. How fucking cool is that, right?

But here's the thing.

Since the bad stuff compounds too, you just have to make sure that the good stuff compounds faster than the bad stuff.

The new kid I told you about told me that.

I think pretty much he should sit with us at lunch from now on.

You do know you still sit with me at lunch, don't you?

65

WHEN THERE WAS NOTHING LEFT

but cinders and ash, Eli said, "I'm going to go out into the world and help as many people as I can."

I said, "I'm going to plant food for the hungry, spread peanut butter as thickly as I want to, take foster kids in when I'm older, and make sure that everyone has socks."

Then Benj said, "I'm going to make friends and not take anyone for granted."

And I said, "I'm going to not judge people, read all the banned books, and embrace the violence of words."

"What about God?" Eli asked.

"That would be a maybe. A *soft* maybe."

Eli smiled through her tears and squeezed my hand. Then I told her there was something that I wanted her to read and I took out my phone.

"There are six hundred and ninety-three text messages that I wrote to you over the past year but never sent. I saved most of them and I want you to read them now."

"You wrote me six hundred and ninety-three messages that you didn't send? Six hundred and ninety-three?" Eli asked.

"Six hundred and ninety-three? Seriously, man?" Benj asked.

"Pretty much that would be a yes."

I opened the *save to draft* file, handed Eli my phone, and in the process opened the door to a car that was careening toward a tractor trailer at high speed with no brakes and I jumped.

But I didn't care.

I just tucked my head, put my shoulder into it, and rolled.

Eli took my phone and walked a few steps away and then sat down on the grass and started scrolling through a one-year conversation she and I never actually had.

And Benj and I watched as the last wisps of smoke trailed up to the sky.

Then Benj said, "This was great, Joel. Thanks again, man."

"It was nothing. We're friends now, remember?"

"You know, we could still go to the real Burning Man."

And I said, "How's the penny project?"

And he said, "Not so good."

Then Benj and I looked over and Eli was crying again.

Benj said, "That move you just did? Brass balls, man."

"I know, right?"

"Yep."

"Which way do you think it will go?"

"Well, it was either the absolute worst fucking idea in the world or the best. She's either going to get a restraining order against you or light up your night sky."

Eli's face was riveted to the screen of my phone and she was reading every one of the crazy-ass, deranged, overly emotional, wholly embarrassing texts that I had typed to her thinking that she would never see them. And you know what?

I was okay with it.

Then Eli walked over and handed me her phone and she said, "Read this, Joel Higgins."

I said, "What is it?"

Benj said, "Probably that restraining order or hate mail."

Eli said, "It's a list."

Then Benj said, "Should have seen *that* coming."

I looked down. The list had a title.

EVERYTHING I LOVE ABOUT JOEL HIGGINS

And it was surrounded by yellow hearts and birthday cake emojis.

I had to read the title five times to make sure that it didn't say EVERYTHING I HATE ABOUT JOEL HIGGINS.

I said, "Is this one of your short lists or long lists?"

And Eli said, "It's the longest list I've ever written."

And then Eli kissed me.

As in, Eli kissed Joel.

AS IN, HER LIPS ON MY MOUTH.

And it was the best thing that ever happened in my entire life.

Possibly the best thing that had ever happened in the whole world.

Ever.

Then Benj said, "You know, now that you two are a couple, the three of us could all go to Burning Man together."

"Not happening, Benj. I have to read the rest of *Winnie-the-Pooh* to Patrick Allen Samson at the VA hospital this summer."

"Okay, how about just me and Eli, then?"

"Not happening, Benj."

"I have a yurt."

"No, you don't."

"Okay, maybe not yet but I will, and you'll see, Joel. You'll change your mind."

"No way."

"Way. Okay, how about the SATs? At least take the SATs."

"Not happening, Benj."

"You'll see. You'll change your mind on both counts."

"No way."

Then Eli said, "Way."

"Way what?"

"You're taking the SATs."

"Okay, maybe in the fall."

Then Benj added, "Wait, do you hear that?"

"Hear what?"

"Ka-ching! It's the pennies compounding," Benj said as he grinned.

And then Eli kissed me again.

And again.

And again.

And I knew that I was going to kiss her back 10.7 million times.

Okay, maybe more.

ACKNOWLEDGMENTS

I would like to thank (in no particular order) A. A. Milne, advocates for freedom and democracy around the world, E. B. White, inspirational teachers, Harper Lee, rebel moms, Shel Silverstein, defenders of free speech, Maya Angelou, librarians everywhere (you rock), Lynne Banks, veterans, wounded warriors, Roald Dahl, the inventor of Haagen-Dazs chocolate peanut butter ice cream, anyone who has ever stood up to injustice and been brave, Astrid Lindgren, small organic farmers, Toni Morrison, seed savers, J. D. Salinger, the people who paved the bike paths in Westchester County, and Sgt. R. Hubert of the Bedford, New York, Police Department for advising me on police protocol. And because no one ever thanks them, I would like to thank all of the AWFUL people in this world (you know who you are) who remind the rest of us every single day that while it's so easy to say and do negative things, it's so much better to say and do—and write—positive and compassionate and forward-moving things.

Also, profound and heartfelt thanks to my husband for all those ink-runs to Staples and for never admitting to being sick of rereading the same material no matter how many times I asked and for digging my sunflower garden every year without complaining and for growing vegetables and fruit and flowers and ideas and children with me and for a lifetime of precious moments too numerous and too personal to mention here. I am also deeply grateful to all three of my children for being the best reading buddies ever—I wouldn't trade the time we had with books for anything—with extra super-special thanks to my daughter, Kate, who lived through the day-to-day writing of this book with me. Thank you for knowing how to spell so many more words than I do and for never getting exasperated and never telling me to stop being so annoying and use spell check and for always asking if I have any new pages to read. Your interest in knowing what happened next was my canary in the coal mine.

Sincere thanks to everyone at Hyperion who advocated for and shaped this project: to Emily Meehan and Julie Rosenberg, whose offer read more like a love letter to Joel and Eli than a business contract. To Hannah Allaman, who adopted the manuscript and dove in headfirst to edit it—you pushed me to make it better. It *is* better. So much better. I am grateful for both your sensitivity to my vision and for your insight and guidance on plot points, scene construction, voice, and character—it was invaluable. Thank you! I also owe a debt of gratitude to the rest of the publishing team: Jacqueline Hornberger for copyediting the manuscript without putting a single punctuation mark in any of the rambling monologues—as tempting as it must have been to do so. Thank you for that, and also for gently pointing out that there aren't eight weeks in a month and that four Stevies in one book is probably three Stevies too many. I would also like to thank Jamie Alloy for designing the best book cover in the history of the world, and everyone—including

Elke Villa, Andrew Sansone, Sara Liebling, Guy Cunningham, Dina Sherman, Amy Goppert, Frank Bumbalo, and Therese Ellis—in marketing and sales and production who helped turn this story into something luminous and alive. I would also like to extend heartfelt thanks to all the booksellers, bloggers, reviewers, and readers who picked up a copy of this book and took valued time away from other things in their lives to read it. As I am sure you already know, you are the most important people in the book universe!

Also, I owe a huge debt of gratitude to my absolutely brilliant agent, Molly O'Neill, who made this book possible in the first place. You are as nurturing as a kindergarten teacher and as tough as a samurai! Thank you for finding me in your inbox and for reading early pages and far too many drafts than I should have asked you to, and for brainstorming with me and making suggestions on plot and narrative arc and structure and character development and for telling me outright when something wasn't working and for finding Joel and Eli such a lovely home and for being so smart and strategic and patient and for teaching me so much and for always explaining the *why*. You are a plot ninja and book agent extraordinaire. Thank you!

And finally, I'd like to thank Joel and Eli and Benj and Alex B. Renner and Jacey. Don't tell anyone, but I think you're real and that I'm your mom. And now that you've gone to live in bookstores with all the other people made out of ink and paper, I'm going to miss you! Just try to make friends with the good kids: with Holden Caulfield and Katniss and Scout Finch and Troy Billings and Hazel Grace and Ponyboy and Liesel and Lotta . . . And always remember that even though we no longer spend all day together, I still sit with you at lunch. And that I still text you! ☺